A real life good samaritan. . .with a quirk.

"How're we doing?"

"We're making good time. I think I'll get there before they close."

"What does this guy do that he couldn't take time off for a regular wedding?"

"Sam's an accountant. It's tax time, you know."

"That figures." He glanced over at her with a raised eyebrow. "I hope you're not looking for a lot of excitement in life. My uncle was an accountant, and his nose was always in a page of figures. I made up my mind I wouldn't live like that."

She started to comment, but decided to let it go. If he wanted to be a truck driver, that was his business.

"I don't suppose it occurred to you to wait until after tax season and get married when school was out, did it?"

"Of course. That was what I wanted to do, but Sam insisted we should get married now, so I finally gave in."

"He was probably afraid he would lose you if he waited."

That had never occurred to her, and she was rather surprised at the idea. "Oh, I don't think so. There was no reason for him to worry about that."

"You never know," he said thoughtfully. "No, you never know what's right around the corner."

She stared at him. What did that mean?

HELEN SPEARS was born and raised in Arkansas and now lives in Tulsa, Oklahoma with her husband (also a writer). She has two sons and a granddaughter. Helen began writing when her sons went off to college. She finds writing inspirational romances quite natural and enjoys the process since she believes God will find a way to reach and teach through love as well as other aspects of life.

Books by Helen Spears

HEARTSONG PRESENTS
HP173—The Hasty Heart

The Reluctant Bride

Helen Spears

Heartsong Presents

To Greg and Chris and Croakie and Froggy

A note from the author:
I love to hear from my readers! You may correspond with me
by writing: **Helen Spears**
Author Relations
PO Box 719
Uhrichsville, OH 44683

ISBN 1-57748-485-1

THE RELUCTANT BRIDE

All Scripture quotations are from the Authorized King James
Version of the Bible unless otherwise noted.

Cover illustration by Adam Wallenta.

PRINTED IN THE U.S.A.

one

Chelsea Morgan made one more effort to stay calm. The mail had come, and there was still nothing from the lab about her blood test. It was ridiculous that it had to be sent to the state capital to be processed. Just having a three-day waiting period was bad enough.

Now she was trying to find out what happened through a highly unsatisfactory long distance phone call. "But I'm getting married tomorrow. I have to have that report."

It didn't help that the voice on the other end of the line was apologetic.

"How could you lose something like that?" She felt her blood pressure rising. Finally, she gave up and replaced the receiver. Panic took the place of the anger. What could she do now?

Quickly, she dialed Sam at his office across the line in North Dakota. Her voice was quavery as she explained her problem to him. "The lab has lost my blood report. Now what do I do?" The minister had been engaged, and her principal had arranged for a substitute for her so that she could take Friday off from her classes at school.

Sam was talking. He had made some kind of gutteral sound of displeasure. "You'll just have to drive over here and get your blood test made. There isn't a waiting period in this state. Call me when you get here. Okay?"

She nodded. Of course, he was so sensible. "Yes, I'll leave just as soon as I can. How long does it take?"

She groaned when he told her forty-five minutes, but what

choice did she have? "Okay, dear. I'll be there as soon as I can." She would be lucky to make it before the lab closed.

She stopped long enough to fill her car up with gas on the way out of town, then she turned onto the wide highway and gained as much speed as her old car could handle. Even at this hour of the day, traffic was sparse.

Thank goodness for that, she thought.

More than ever, she was regretting that she had let Sam rush her. Not that she didn't want to marry him. Of course, she did. He was very much in love with her, and very attractive. Any girl would be thrilled to have him. He had arrived in town and swept her off her feet before she even had a chance to catch her breath. She thought back. How long had it been now? About four months if she remembered correctly.

There hadn't even been anyone in Stanville whom she wanted to date, much less marry. Then Sam showed up and started courting her. She would have preferred to wait until school was out, but he managed to persuade her to get married. Chelsea's mother had insisted she should have a traditional wedding with all the fuss, but even she relented when she met Sam. She realized he was a good catch, and she was impatient to have a grandchild.

Chelsea tuned in the radio and sang along with the music as she drove. Every so often she would check the clock on the dashboard. She would make it with time to spare. She relaxed a bit, and then the car gave a strange little cough.

There was nothing but bare, flat farmland as far as the eye could see. Not even a house broke the monotony of the drive between the two towns, and she was about halfway there by now. A late afternoon watery sun did nothing to warm up the cold landscape. Chelsea snapped off the radio and strained her ear to hear any more unusual noises from the engine.

Soon there was another cough, and the motor started missing.

What could be wrong? Now the car slowed until it was barely moving. She pulled over to the side of the road and tried to gun the motor, but it just coughed again and stopped.

Now what? she wondered.

She tried to be calm, reminding herself of her favorite Bible verse. "We know that all things work together for good to them that love God, to them who are the called according to his purpose." *It's hard to see how this can be good for me,* she reasoned.

She sat there for at least fifteen minutes before the first car whizzed by, not even slowing out of curiosity. After another ten minutes or so, another car came by, slowing slightly, then regaining speed and disappearing in the distance.

She sighed. She couldn't get out and walk. It was too far to town. She supposed if she stayed there long enough, Sam would get worried about her and come after her, but by that time she would have missed her chance to get her lab work done, and the wedding would have to be postponed.

For a brief moment she was swept by the same desolate feeling she had experienced at the age of sixteen when her beloved father had died.

Just then, she heard the powerful sound of a big semi approaching. Feeling absolutely desperate, she opened her door and got out, waving at the huge truck.

She heard the sound of the air brakes taking hold. Thank goodness he was stopping. A tall, well-built man with dark hair and warm blue eyes hopped out of the cab and strode toward her. "What's wrong, ma'am? You got car trouble?"

"Yes." She nodded. "It stopped on me, and I'm in a terrible hurry to get to New Mill."

He climbed into her car and tried to start it. It turned over once, then died. He got out and looked under the hood, then shook his head. "Looks like more trouble than I can handle here. You're going to need a mechanic. Lock it up, and I'll give you a lift."

He went back to his truck and got in the driver's seat, and Chelsea followed as quickly as she could, hobbling in the long, tight skirt which made it impossible to walk fast. Of course, her mother had warned her all her life never to get in the car with a stranger, but she couldn't have anticipated this kind of situation.

The driver turned from his seat and called through the open window. "You got some kind of problem down there, lady? Let's go."

Chelsea could have just barely climbed into that high cab wearing jeans. With her tight skirt, it was quite impossible. "I'm sorry," she yelled, "I can't manage this in my tight skirt."

She heard his sigh as he got out of the truck and came around to her side, looking ever so superior and amused. She quickly looked away, hoping to hide her embarrassment.

Cupping his hands under her hips, he boosted her up into the cab. She made a firm resolve to donate that skirt to Goodwill as soon as she got back home.

So this was the way a truck looked inside. She took in her unaccustomed surroundings. It seemed everything was scaled extra-large to go with the size of the huge van attached to the rear.

Western music twanged on the radio, and Chelsea stole a glance at the driver. Nice profile. Firm chin, ruddy complexion, dark hair, almost black, carelessly combed once and let fall any which way. The contrast of his eyes, the warmest blue she had ever seen, was his most striking feature. He had a nice build, too. Firm and lean, with wide shoulders.

Actually, she liked what she saw, but of course, she wouldn't have anything in common with a trucker. Furthermore, he probably wouldn't be attracted to her looks. She could already tell by the way he addressed her. A trucker would certainly like someone much flashier, a blond with long hair, instead of a brown-eyed brunette with short brown hair. And, of course, men these days liked very tall, slim girls, and she was just average. Not that it mattered. Sam liked her well enough. Besides, she had been football queen in college, so she knew she was attractive.

The Western music ended and a commercial came on. The trucker glanced her way and became aware she was looking him over. He reached across and turned down the radio. "So, what's the rush to get to New Mill?"

"I have to take care of an urgent matter. I need to stop at the City Hospital Lab." She checked a card with the address on it which she fished out of her purse. "It's at 314 South Main. I don't suppose you'll be going that way, will you?"

"Sure. I go right by it. I'll be glad to drop you off." He was quiet for a moment, then curiosity got the better of him. "It's none of my business, but are you suffering from some kind of illness? I mean, you look pretty healthy to me."

She hesitated. It really was none of his business, but he had been good to stop. "Nothing like that. You see, I'm getting married tomorrow, and I thought I'd had my blood test done in plenty of time back at Stanville, but something went wrong, and they lost it. Now, I'm in a jam. If I can't get to the lab before they close, and convince them I need the results by noon tomorrow, well, I'll just have to postpone the wedding."

He frowned. "Mmmm. You are in a jam." He gave her a look of concern. "If it had been up to me, I never would have let that happen. You know, you have to sit on those bureaucracies, state labs, and such, and make sure they come across. Yes sir, I'm surprised the fellow you're marrying didn't make sure all those details were in order."

"Well, I'm sure he felt he could leave it up to me. I certainly don't blame him."

"So, are you having a big wedding? White gown, and all that?"

She laughed, but her expression was wistful. "Oh, no. It's just going to be a simple ceremony with our best friends standing up for us. There was no time to have a big affair, even if we had wanted it."

"That's a shame. You know, you look like the kind of a woman who should have a traditional wedding with all the trimmings."

"I always thought so, but. . ." Her voice cracked, and he gave her a sharp look. Then she continued as if nothing had happened. "There was no way we could get off work long enough for that. Sam is very busy with his business right now, and I had a hard enough time persuading my principal to arrange for a substitute so I could have a long weekend off."

"You're a schoolteacher?"

"Yes. I teach third grade."

"I'll bet you're a good teacher, too."

"I hope so. I really like it. The children are very impressionable at that age, and I feel that what I do is important to them."

"Yeah, I'm sure you're right." His mouth turned up in a wry little smile. "Boy, you sure don't look like my third-grade teacher."

"I don't?"

"No. Miss Eubanks was at least fifty, tall and straight up and down. Believe me, she wasn't much fun."

"That's too bad. I believe children learn better if they're enjoying the process."

"Of course they do." He was silent for a moment, and she checked her watch. There was still time. These trucks went awfully fast.

"How're we doing?"

"We're making good time. I think I'll get there before they close."

"What does this guy do that he couldn't take time off for a regular wedding?"

"Sam's an accountant. It's tax time, you know."

"That figures." He glanced over at her with a raised eyebrow. "I hope you're not looking for a lot of excitement in life. My uncle was an accountant, and his nose was always in a page of figures. I made up my mind I wouldn't live like that."

She started to comment, but decided to let it go. If he wanted to be a truck driver, that was his business.

"I don't suppose it occurred to you to wait until after tax season and get married when school was out, did it?"

"Of course. That was what I wanted to do, but Sam insisted we should get married now, so I finally gave in."

"He was probably afraid he would lose you if he waited."

That had never occurred to her, and she was rather surprised at the idea. "Oh, I don't think so. There was no reason for him to worry about that."

"You never know," he said thoughtfully. "No, you never know what's right around the corner."

She stared at him. What did that mean? It reminded her of a magazine article she read when she was fifteen and bored to death. It was called "The Law of Surprises," and showed by examples of true incidents how when you least expected it surprises came along to change your life.

They were nearing New Mill, the small town that would soon be her home. Like many small towns, it was built around its leading industry. Founded by Herbert Van Oghden, whose feed mill supported most of the families thereabout, it was now a thriving oasis in this sparsely populated state. The Van Oghden mansion had been built only about twenty years ago, and gave the town a bit of much-needed class.

The trucker's voice interrupted Chelsea's reverie. "Well, we're almost there. New Mill's about a mile down the road. I'll just drop you off at the hospital, and I hope everything goes well for you, Miss. . . ?"

"Morgan. Chelsea Morgan. Sorry, I forgot to introduce myself. And you're?"

"Greg McCormick." Now he pulled over in front of the hospital, leaned across her, and opened the door. "Look, if anything. . .I mean, if you. . . Well, never mind. Good luck."

"I can't thank you enough." She looked down at the ground, which seemed ever so far away. Should she jump out with both feet?

He noticed her hesitancy and quickly hurried around to her side. Reaching up with both hands, he helped her down. "You really should make a slit in that skirt," he observed. "Well, so long."

"Good-bye, and thanks again." She glanced at her watch and walked as fast as she could to the lab. She was ushered right in to have her blood test done, but had the distinct impression the lab technician didn't feel the same urgency she did to get the results out by her deadline of noon tomorrow.

As she left, she turned and repeated her explanation of why she was in a rush for her test results, then she walked the two blocks to Sam's office.

His secretary, the loyal and faithful Dolores, had already gone home, although it wasn't unusual for her to stay late whenever it was necessary. Sam was still sitting in his office going over his papers. He didn't look up when she walked in, and for a minute she stood there and looked at him.

He's a good-looking man, she thought. Blond hair, neatly combed, handsome clothes, an overall look of well-kept middle America. His blond good looks reminded her of her father, whom she had adored.

She cleared her throat, and he looked up. "Oh, hello, dear." He gave her a warm smile. "Did you get the blood test made?"

"Yes, it's all taken care of. I just hope they'll get it out in time."

"So do I. Maybe you'd better give them a ring in the morning and remind them you need it."

"Are you about ready to leave?"

"Yes. Just give me a couple of minutes more." He returned to his work, and she sat down to wait, feeling frustrated. She hadn't had a chance to tell him about her car.

Finally, he put aside his work and rose from his desk, stretching. "Sorry about that. I couldn't find a good stopping place. Shall we go eat?"

"Sam, there's one more thing. My car broke down on the way over here."

"It did? Well, how did you get here?"

"I hitched a ride with a trucker."

He gave her a sharp look. "You *what?* A trucker? Are you insane?" He took out his phone directory and thumbed through it. "I'd better call the station where I take my car. Maybe they can send someone out."

She waited while he talked to an attendant, then he replaced the receiver and turned to her. "Give me your keys. Someone will tow it in tonight."

"Good." She reached in her purse and found her keys, which she handed to him. "Now, let's go eat. I'm starved."

They started toward the door, and he put his hand out to open it, then he stopped and reached for her. Putting his arms around her, he kissed her lightly on the lips. "Just one more day, honey. Just one more day!"

She smiled. "Yes, it seems as if things are getting awfully hectic, doesn't it? I mean the blood test, and the car, and your

work, and Mr. Culpepper. He wasn't too happy about giving
me time off right now."

"Well, you know you could always quit. You don't have to
have that job."

"Now, Sam, we've been all through that." They walked out
to his car. "You know I want to keep my job. I like teaching.
It's important to me."

He started the motor and pulled away from the curb. His
voice sounded resigned. "Yes, I know. I was just hoping you
would change your mind, at least for a while."

"It doesn't work that way. If you're a teacher, you teach.
You don't dabble. After all, you wouldn't consider quitting
your job for a while, would you?"

"Of course not, but that's different."

"I don't see why. Your work is important to you, and my
work is important to me." She turned and smiled at him.
"Well, let's not argue tonight. Not on the eve of our wedding."

His answering smile made her feel better.

They stopped at their favorite local restaurant, the Pines,
and were greeted cordially by Glenn, the owner, who was
always on hand to see that everything ran well. He seemed
especially pleased to see them, since they usually came only
on the weekends.

"Welcome." He spoke to Sam. "You're looking awfully
happy tonight. Is this a special occasion?"

Chelsea couldn't resist. "We're getting married tomorrow."

Glenn's response was effusive. "Well, congratulations. I
insist you must try this special appetizer we just introduced
this week. Compliments of the house."

They were seated at their usual corner table. Sam held her
chair, and told her she looked lovely tonight. "You're the
prettiest woman in the room."

The waiter brought their appetizers, two small plates of

oysters, cooked three ways, served in their shells. "Glenn has outdone himself with these," Sam remarked after sampling an oyster Rockefeller.

Chelsea nodded. "Yes, this is superb." She asked him about his day.

"Another tough day with the tax forms," he said, "but I have it about whipped by now. I'll spend a few more hours on it after I get back from taking you home, then I'll be ready to take some time off."

"I guess we should have waited until school was out," she said. "We're really pushing ourselves, aren't we?"

His jaw set stubbornly. "No, I don't think it would be any easier. There's always work to be done. You just have to decide to do something, then do it. This is as good a time as any." That seemed to end that topic as far as he was concerned, so she let it drop.

She didn't think about it again until they were on the road driving toward Stanville. "There it is," she said as they passed her stalled car. It was very depressing, and it made her realize how hectic tomorrow would be. "I don't know how I'll manage to get around in the morning."

"You'll just have to call Ginnie and tell her what your problem is. I'm sure she'll drive you wherever you need to go." Ginnie was her best friend, who was planning to be her only attendant at the wedding.

"Yes, I guess that's all I can do."

It was still early when Sam drove up to her apartment. He walked in with her and kissed her warmly at the door. "I'd better run, honey. I need to get back and wind up my work. Tomorrow will be here before we know it." He kissed her again, then hurriedly walked down the hall.

Chelsea locked the door behind her, then crossed over to the telephone. She nervously drummed the table as she waited for Ginnie to answer, then at the sound of the familiar voice, she relaxed a bit.

"This is the bride speaking, and I have a bit of a problem."

"Nothing serious, I hope."

Chelsea explained about the blood test and the car.

"Wow, you do have problems." Her voice was full of sympathy. "I'm at your service, so call me as soon as you know anything. I'll be glad to drive you anywhere you want to go, or run any errands. That's what the maid of honor is for, you know."

"Thanks. I knew I could count on you. Well, I'm bushed. It's been a hectic day. I think I'll turn in." Chelsea replaced the receiver and got ready for bed.

Her prayer that night was brief. *Dear Lord, I know that all things work together for good to them that love God, and I must say I feel a bit out of control after all that has happened today. Please bless me on the eve of my wedding, and help it all to turn out for the best. Amen.*

She turned on her bedside lamp and picked up the half-finished book she was reading. She was really tired. As she read, the words began to blur on the page, and soon a pair of warm, blue eyes stared back at her.

two

Chelsea woke to the sound of sleet hitting her window. She quickly closed her eyes, dreading the drive to school, not ready to face the day. Then she remembered. She sat bolt upright, every nerve tingling. This was her wedding day!

Hadn't she read somewhere that it was perfectly normal for every bride to have last-minute doubts? Was she doing the right thing? Now she was facing the worst case of nerves she had ever had. Did Sam feel the same way?

She threw back the covers and slipped her feet into her fuzzy slippers. If only the sun were shining. It would make all the difference in the world. She slipped her warm flannel robe on, and went in to splash cold water on her face.

She wanted to call Ginnie, but it was still too early. That would have to wait. She went into the kitchen and filled the coffeepot, poured cereal into a bowl, and drank a glass of orange juice. Glancing at the clock, she saw that it was only 6:30.

After pouring a cup of coffee, she turned on the TV. The weather report should be on right after the commercial. She had to know how long this early spring storm would last.

She sipped her coffee and sat on the edge of the sofa watching as the weatherman pointed to the map. "More sleet and icy weather is coming in on top of the present storm," he said. "The highway patrol is urging all citizens to stay off the highways except for emergencies," he continued.

She set her cup down, and went into the kitchen, where she poured milk on her cereal and stood looking out the window while she ate it. The ground was already white, and gusts of wind from the north eddied the sleet around the shrubs.

Chelsea returned to the TV where the newscaster was just finishing an item about a storm-related accident. ". . .And the driver of the semi was unconscious when he was taken to the hospital. . . . In Washington, D.C., the president. . ." She snapped off the set and took her empty cup back to the kitchen. With shaking hands, she refilled it.

Sternly she lectured herself as she drank the hot coffee. *There must be hundreds of truck drivers out on the road this morning. It could have been any of them. There's absolutely no reason to think it could have been Greg McCormick.*

She continued her lecture. *It's amazing you remembered his name. After all, you only met him once. Now, it's time to get busy. You're supposed to get married today.*

She went to the telephone and called Sam. Good, he was still at home. His voice sounded strong and determined. "Glad you called, honey. I was just getting ready to call you. How is the weather there?"

"Terrible. I just had the news on, and there has already been a bad accident. The highway patrol says no one should be on the highways."

"Yeah, I know. I've already called them. It's sleeting here, too. We'll have to postpone the wedding."

He sounded terribly depressed.

"It's such a shame," she said. "I had no idea it was going to be so bad today. I hope you won't be too unhappy."

"Yeah, well I'm just sick about it, but what can we do? Will you call everyone there? We'll just have to reset it once the storm is over. It sounds like it could last for days."

"Yes, I'll take care of it. I guess I'll have to manage without my car, too. Have they towed it in yet?"

"Yes, they towed it in last night. Sorry about all this, honey. I love you."

"You, too." She replaced the receiver and took a deep breath. The tension seemed to drain out of her. She checked the clock and decided to wait thirty minutes before making her calls. It was still awfully early.

She returned to the living room and turned the TV back on. The local news was on again with more information on the storm. She sat there watching, hoping there would be another report on the injured truck driver. There was no more local news, though.

She paced the floor restlessly, then went back to the telephone. That report had been on the local news. It was just possible he could be in the Stanville Hospital.

She looked up the number in the phone book. She was just curious, that was all. No one would know she had called. Now the switchboard was answering.

"Yes, do you have a Greg McCormick who was recently admitted?"

"One moment, please." There was a brief silence. "Yes, ma'am, Mr. McCormick was admitted early this morning."

"Could you tell me what his condition is? I'm a friend."

"He's listed in good condition. Just a moment, I'll connect you."

"No. . .I just. . ."

But it was too late; his voice was already on the line.

"Oh, I didn't mean to bother you. She just connected us." This was so embarrassing. He must think she was an idiot. "This is Chelsea Morgan. I saw the story about your accident on the news this morning. I was just checking to see how you were."

"Well, I'll be. It's the bride." He chuckled. "That's real nice of you. I'm just fine. I'll be out of here this afternoon."

"I'm glad to hear it. Well, I'd better let you get some rest."

"Wait. Don't be in such a rush. I guess you'll have to postpone the wedding, won't you?"

"Yes. I just talked to Sam. The roads are impassable, so of course, there's no way we could have the wedding today."

"Of course not." He sounded sympathetic. "That's too bad. No telling how long this will last."

"No telling. There won't be a wedding this weekend. Where will you go when you get out of the hospital?"

"I'll find a room, I guess. I have to see about my load, too. It'll just have to be late. Can't be helped, you know. So, what will you do today?"

"I have to make a few telephone calls to the people involved in the wedding. My car is in a garage in New Mill, so I'm without transportation, too." She sighed. "Not that it matters. I couldn't go anywhere today, anyway."

"No, I suppose not. It's not a great day for either of us, is it?"

"No, but I'm glad you're okay at least."

"Yeah, well thanks for calling. Take care."

She replaced the receiver and sat there smiling rather foolishly. His face blazed as clear in her mind as if he'd been in the room with her.

He's okay. He's okay. The words sounded over and over in her thoughts, and suddenly she felt energized.

She went to her room and dressed, then she returned to the telephone and called the minister, the florist, and Ginnie, who sounded terribly concerned.

"Oh, you poor dear! I am so sorry. You must be terribly disappointed."

"Yes. We'll just have to reset it." Then, she made a decision quite unexpectedly. "I've decided to postpone the wedding until after school is out."

There was a moment's silence, then Ginnie's voice sounded

puzzled. "You have?"

"Yes. This has all been too hectic. We'll be married in June when we have time for a proper wedding."

"Does Sam know about this?"

"Not yet, but he'll just have to go along with me. I'm sure I can make him see reason."

"I hope so. Well, let me know if I can do anything for you. Do you need for me to make any phone calls?"

"No, thanks. I've already taken care of that."

Chelsea replaced the receiver and went back to look out the window. The sleet was coming down in angry waves now, turning the landscape white and hitting the windows like hundreds of bird claws. Thank goodness she didn't have to go out in this.

Her sudden decision to postpone her wedding until the end of the semester had come as a surprise, but it seemed like a reasonable response to the events of the last few days.

Her first impulse was to call Sam and tell him how she felt, and she went back to the telephone and picked it up, but she quickly replaced it. Sam would be at the office, working. Never mind that there was a blizzard. If he couldn't drive, he would walk the few blocks from his apartment to his office building. She replaced the receiver. It would be best to tell him in person.

She spent the rest of the day finishing the book she was reading and cleaning out her kitchen cabinets. By the time she went to bed, the storm had let up.

The wind shifted during the night, and the next morning dawned with a clear, cold sun sparkling on the ice. By noon, the sleet had started to melt, and by the end of the day, there was only dirty slush in the streets.

Chelsea talked to Sam on the telephone twice, purposely being vague about resetting their wedding date. She still wanted to tell him in person what she had in mind. He would have driven over, but she didn't encourage him. "Call me as soon as my car is ready, and I'll see if I can get Ginnie to drive me over." That seemed to satisfy him, and they left it at that.

Sunday morning dawned cold and sloppy, with a lot of dirty slush still on the streets. Chelsea dressed for church, wearing boots, a heavy coat with a hood, and mittens. The attendance would be sparse, but she had an urge to be there. It would be an oasis of calm in her upset weekend.

She put her Bible in her pocket and set out to trudge the two blocks to the church. As long as the wind didn't blow too hard, she could stand it.

Reverend Sanders was glad to see her, greeting her warmly. "Too bad about your bad luck weather-wise. Let me know when you're ready to reset the wedding."

"Thanks, I will."

As far as Dr. Sanders's sermon was concerned, the church could have been standing room only. He gave it his all, as he always did.

Chelsea had been brought up in a Christian household, and she still adhered to her principles, attending church regularly, belonging to a Bible study group and a prayer circle. When her Aunt Joanne became ill with cancer, she saw to it that her name was added to the list of people for whom her group prayed.

By the time the church service was over, Chelsea felt much more relaxed. She stopped to visit with a few of the hearty souls who had ventured out that morning.

Ginnie called as she was getting ready for bed that night and offered to drop her off at school in the morning.

"You're a dear," Chelsea said. "I'd really appreciate it."

"Is 8:30 too early?"

"Not at all," Chelsea replied. "I usually go early and have a roll and coffee in the teachers' lounge with my friends."

She thanked Ginnie again, and replaced the receiver.

Everyone should have a friend like Ginnie, she reflected as she turned out the light. She and Ginnie had come forward to be baptized together at an evangelical meeting. They had been friends ever since.

Chelsea's prayer was brief that night. *Thank You, Lord, for the wintery storm. I know it was the sign I needed to tell me I should postpone my wedding so I could do it properly. Thank You for my friend Ginnie. I realize she is one in a million.* She hesitated briefly, then continued. *And thank You for helping Greg McCormick to be okay after his accident. Amen.*

By morning, there was little trace left of the big spring storm. The weatherman on TV promised several days of slowly warming temperatures. Chelsea happily dressed for school and grabbed her briefcase as soon as she heard Ginnie's car outside.

"I worried about you being depressed over the weekend," Ginnie told her as they drove toward the schoolhouse. "I'm glad to see you looking so cheerful this morning."

"Oh, you needn't have worried. Actually, I believe things usually work out for the best, even though we don't always recognize the possibility at the time. I just hope Sam wasn't too depressed."

"Yes. Poor guy. He must have been crushed. What did he say when you told him you were postponing the wedding until June?"

"Well, you see, I haven't told him yet. I thought it would be best to wait and tell him in person."

"Yes, I expect you're right." Ginnie pulled her car up to the curb in front of the school.

"Thanks loads," Chelsea said as she climbed out of the car. "See you later." She hurried into the school building, anxious to see her fellow teachers after having been shut in most of the weekend by the storm.

As she pushed open the door to the teachers' lounge, she found herself in one of the most embarrassing situations of her entire life. She was greeted by the sounds of a dozen voices singing "Here Comes the Bride." Someone had scrounged up an old, scratchy recording of the wedding music to accompany them. Instead of the usual coffee and sweet rolls, there was a decorated cake and a bowl of punch.

Even Mr. Culpepper, the principal, had joined the party, looking a bit out of place and awkward. At least he had the good sense not to try to sing, Chelsea observed.

She stood there, wishing she could go through the floor, until they finished singing, then she blinked and swallowed. It was a moment she would never forget.

Trying to appear gracious, she thanked them and explained how the storm had forced them to cancel the ceremony. Once Mr. Culpepper left, everyone seemed more relaxed, and there were jokes about how they couldn't keep having celebrations unless she was willing to actually have a wedding.

After that, she managed to slip into her usual routine, the only problem being the difficulty of keeping order after the students had enjoyed a rather exciting weekend.

By the end of the school day, she was relieved to hear the final bell. Once the pupils had cleared the room, she gathered up her materials and started down the hall, forgetting for the moment that she had no transportation.

She pushed open the heavy front door and was greeted by a sight that set her heart pounding. There, parked right in front and looking about as big as the *Queen Mary,* was Greg McCormick's semi.

three

Chelsea was wearing a pleated skirt that made it easy for her to take the steep step into the cab of the big semi. As she opened the door to enter, she heard a deep voice behind her.

"I didn't know your young man was a truck driver," Mr. Culpepper said.

Chelsea swung her head around, gave him a startled look, and hopped back down.

"I was just on my way to my car," he explained. "I'd like to meet him."

"Well, er. . ." she stammered, wondering how to explain.

Now Greg had come around, and quickly assessed the situation as Chelsea grappled for words to introduce him. He thrust his hand out to shake Mr. Culpepper's hand heartily. "Glad to meet you, sir. Chelsea's mentioned you before. Actually, I'm just a family friend, passing through town."

Chelsea gave a sigh of relief as her principal bid them goodbye and went on his way. "That was quick thinking," she said, climbing into the cab of the truck. As Greg took his seat beside her, she gave him a quick once-over. "Are you all right?"

"Yeah, fine. They just wanted to check me for a concussion."

"What happened?"

He had started the engine and pulled out into the street. "I'd stopped to help a motorist when another car slid into my truck, which I was leaning against. The impact knocked me down, and my head hit the ice real hard, causing a concussion." He turned to her. "Which way is your home?"

"It's down this street, then I'll tell you where to turn." She

25

watched as he drove, thinking he looked rather pale. He was probably not as well as he said. "Turn right at the next corner and go two blocks."

"I was afraid you would be riding home with another teacher and I'd miss you altogether."

"No, a friend drove me to school this morning, and to tell you the truth, I'd forgotten I didn't have any transportation. I was glad to see you out there."

He seemed pleased by this. "Don't let me miss my next turn."

"Slow down. It's the red brick apartment house on the right in the next block."

He pulled the semi up to the curb in front of the apartment building.

"Thanks." She opened the door. *Yes, he definitely looks pale,* she thought. "Would you like a cup of coffee before you go on your way?"

"That would just hit the spot." He shut off the engine and climbed out.

They went up the stairs to the second floor, and Chelsea unlocked the door and preceded him into the room.

He glanced around and nodded appreciatively. "Nice," he said. "Good colors."

"Thanks." She smiled at his unexpected comment. It had taken a lot of nerve to paint the walls mustard yellow, but it was what had made the room come alive with her peach pillows and her blue and white porcelain collection. "Make yourself comfortable while I make the coffee."

She returned with the coffee and found him looking over the books in her bookshelves.

"Nice selection of reading material."

"Now you know. I'm a dyed-in-the-wool bookworm." She motioned toward the sofa. "Sit down and relax," she urged. "Are you sure you feel okay?"

"Oh, sure." He did as she suggested, and she handed him a steaming cup of coffee.

"Cream or sugar?"

"No, thanks." He sipped it at once, and she noticed his hand was not quite steady.

"Isn't your load going to be awfully late?"

"I called one of the guys from the office in New Mill to come take over. We switched trailers and I'll drive his back later on tonight."

She watched as he drank his coffee, waiting to see if his color returned. "Did your doctor say it was all right to go on the road tonight?"

"Well, not exactly. He just said to rest up until I felt strong enough, and he wanted to check me once more. That isn't necessary, though. It takes more than a little blow to the head to put me away." He drained his coffee cup, and she poured more. "Enough about me," he said. "When is that wedding taking place?"

"Not for a while." She poured more coffee into her cup. "I've decided to postpone it until school is out. It won't be until June."

He gave her a sharp look. "Is that right? Not until June. And how about what's-his-name? Is he agreeable to that?"

"Oh, he doesn't know yet. I wanted to wait and tell him in person."

"Yes, I'm sure that would be best. He just might not want to go along."

She winced. "Everything has been so hectic, I just can't go through with another weekend like this. I've made up my mind. We'll have it in June when we can do it properly and invite all our friends and relatives."

There was real concern in Greg's voice. "Well, good for you, but you'd better brace yourself, because I have a feeling your fella is going to give you plenty of pressure to marry him sooner."

"Oh, he will. I'm sure of that." She sighed, dreading the inevitable confrontation.

Greg set his cup down on the saucer, and it rattled noticeably when it touched.

A frown puckered Chelsea's brow as she gave him an appraising glance. "Did you have anything for lunch?"

He thought for a moment. "You know, I believe I forgot to eat. I was so anxious to get my load on its way, I just didn't think about it." He chuckled softly. "That's not like me at all. I'm usually thinking about my next meal." He rose as if to go.

"Look," Chelsea said quickly, "why don't I fix a bite to eat before you go. We'll call it high tea."

He grinned ruefully. "Just the thing. We truckers always stop for tea. I could use a little something, though, if it's not too much trouble."

"Not at all. I'll just be a minute." She went into the kitchen and heated some soup, then she sliced some good French bread to go with it.

Returning to the living room, she motioned for him to come into the dinette. "I have just the thing if you'd care to join me in here."

"Ah, that smells good." He tasted the steaming hot soup. "I didn't realize I was so hungry."

"Where were you headed before the accident?"

"Ames, Iowa. Not too long a haul. Sometimes I go clear across the country and end up in Texas. It's an interesting life."

"You do like it, then."

"Sure. I don't believe in doing what you don't enjoy. Of course, I don't spend all my time on the road. Actually, it's less than you'd think."

"What else do you do?"

"I spend quite a bit of time in the office, out of necessity. After a while, though, I have to hit the open road." His eyes were expressive as he gazed into hers, revealing how much he loved the freedom of the road.

After they had finished their light meal, he started to leave once more. Chelsea noticed his color still hadn't returned. "Do you feel better now?"

"Yes, that was just what I needed." He turned to go back to the living room.

Chelsea was watching him carefully now, wondering if he had recovered sufficiently to drive. As she watched, he swayed almost imperceptibly. "Are you sure you want to start out tonight?"

"Yes, I need to get back," he said, starting toward the door. "Thanks for everything."

This time she knew she hadn't imagined it. He swayed once more, grabbing onto a table. "Greg, why don't you relax a little while longer before you start back," she urged. "Just sit down on the sofa and read the paper while I put these dishes away."

He didn't argue. "Guess I didn't get enough sleep last night," he murmured, sinking into the soft comfort of the sofa.

Chelsea took the dirty dishes into the kitchen and put them in the dishwasher. It took only a few minutes to clear everything up. While she did so, she considered the problem of her guest. It was obvious to her he was in no condition to be out on the road, but could she convince him of that?

She wiped off the table, rinsed the dishcloth, and hung it up, then she returned to the living room, prepared for an argument.

Greg lay sound asleep on the sofa, his long legs draped half on and half off. The paper lay scattered on the floor at his fingertips.

So much for the argument, she thought, spreading a warm afghan over him.

As she straightened, she heard a light tap at her door. Crossing quickly, she opened it to find Ginnie standing there with her cake plate.

"Hi." Ginnie held out the cake plate. "I was on my way home from Mother's when I remembered I'd been meaning to return this." She stepped inside, as always, and turned to Chelsea. "Are you busy?"

"Uh, well. . ."

"I can't stay a minute. I have some. . ." Ginnie was heading for the sofa when she stopped in her tracks. Her big, round eyes stared at Chelsea with astonishment. "Who is that?"

Chelsea put her fingers to her mouth, gesturing for silence, and led Ginnie to the kitchen, where she closed the door. "He's a. . .a friend, Greg McCormick. He was passing through town. I gave him a bite to eat, and he fell asleep while I was doing the dishes."

Ginnie looked at her with a quizzical expression. "I never heard you mention him." She looked at her watch. "It's only a little after five. Kind of early to be going to sleep, don't you think?"

"Would you like a cup of coffee? I'd better explain all this."

"Sure." They sat at the little kitchen table, and Ginnie started questioning her about Greg.

"Where does this guy live?"

"New Mill." Chelsea sipped her coffee and waited for the next question.

"Does Sam know him?"

"I don't think so." She could tell this puzzled Ginnie.

"That's strange. New Mill isn't very large. I should think they would know each other. What does he do?"

Chelsea sighed. "He's a truck driver."

Ginnie's eyes widened. "A truck driver?"

Chelsea was amused by her friend's curiosity. "It's like this, Ginnie. The other day when I drove over to New Mill my car gave out in the middle of nowhere, about halfway there, and I really felt stranded. Finally, this fellow in a big semi came along and stopped."

"You mean this guy here?"

"Yes. He looked under the hood and said he couldn't fix it, so he gave me a lift into town in his truck."

"So, how does he happen to be here now?"

Chelsea explained about his concussion and her accidentally being put through to him when she called the hospital to inquire.

Ginnie seemed amazed at what all had happened. "That's quite a story," she said.

"Yes, I agree. It was just a series of coincidences. Each time I never expected to see him again. I just hope he's all right."

"Well, I didn't mean to pry. I was just curious." She set her cup down and rose. "I'd better run along."

Chelsea didn't urge her to stay. As they passed the sleeping form on the sofa, she noticed Ginnie peered closely at him. Chelsea opened the door and stepped outside with her friend, closing it behind her.

"He's a handsome fellow," Ginnie said with a twinkle.

"Oh, I hadn't noticed. By the way, I don't suppose I could persuade you to drive me over to get my car after school tomorrow."

Ginnie thought for a moment. "I can't think of anything I have to do. Sure, I'd be glad to."

"Thanks. I'll treat you to dinner at Barcarolle."

"You've got a deal."

Chelsea closed the door and returned to the living room. She took a good look at Greg, who hadn't moved since she'd put the afghan over him. What if he were seriously ill, suffering from a concussion? Perhaps she should call the hospital. She leaned closer. He was breathing regularly and, if anything, his color was a little better.

She relaxed. He was all right. As she watched, he stirred and moved his head. His dark hair was tousled, and dark lashes fringed his closed eyes. Ginnie had been right. He was very handsome.

She straightened abruptly. She was engaged to be married, and she had math papers to grade. She picked up her briefcase and went to the bedroom, where she spent the rest of the evening grading papers and preparing her assignments for the next day.

Before she got ready for bed, she tiptoed in to check on Greg once more. He had turned over, and the afghan had slipped off. Other than that, he looked just the same, and the sound of his regular breathing was reassuring. She picked up the afghan and draped it over him, then returned to her bedroom and closed the door.

&

Greg awoke around midnight, wrote a note to Chelsea, and quietly slipped out. A jumble of feelings warred inside him. He was definitely attracted to her, a feeling which he rejected immediately. Surely he was too smart to fall for a woman who was engaged to another man.

Still, her unhappiness was quite evident to him. He needed to know this man. Could he really be as unsuitable as Greg suspected? If she had somehow become trapped in a situation that would ruin her life, he had a strong urge to rescue her.

&

The next morning, Chelsea found a note on her breakfast table. "Thanks for everything," signed Greg in a large masculine scrawl.

The sun was already shining, and she felt so good she decided to walk the mile and a half to school. First, though, she had to call Sam and tell him she would be over to pick up her car.

It was quite early, but he sounded as if he had been up for hours. "I was hoping you'd be over soon. The car is all ready. They replaced some worn part. It's on the bill." He seemed to be in a good mood. "I'll be expecting you then. We have plans to make, you know."

"Yes, we need to talk about that. See you this evening."

And so it starts, she mused. *He's already thinking of resetting the date.* She hoped this wouldn't lead to a scene. She sighed and picked up her briefcase. Outside, the sun had already gone behind a cloud, and the walk to school was decidedly chilly.

The school day passed uneventfully, except for one of Jimmy Preston's typical accidents. Jimmy was accident-prone, and at least once a week he managed to stumble into some sort of mayhem.

This morning he was innocently opening his notebook to insert some new paper, when he managed to mangle his finger on the open notebook ring. Blood covered his desk and streaked his clothes. Pam Holt, sitting behind him, fainted at the sight of all the blood and hit her head, causing more blood to gush forth. Her best friend, Cindy Barron, had a screaming fit, and Mr. Culpepper came down to investigate.

"What's this, Chelsea?" he demanded brusquely, "the start of World War III?"

By the time the final bell rang, Chelsea felt as if she had been in World War III. The walk home helped her unwind, and she was fairly calm by the time Ginnie pulled up in front of her building and honked.

On the highway, heading for New Mill, Chelsea told her

friend all about her day. "You're lucky being a librarian," she said. "I'm sure nothing like that ever happens at the library."

"Well, not often. About the worst thing that happens is an occasional fussy child who has a mild tantrum."

Chelsea nodded. "Yes, I know what you mean."

"What about your handsome friend?" Ginnie asked.

"Greg? He was gone when I got up this morning. He left me a note thanking me for everything and wishing me good luck."

"Maybe you'll see him when we're in New Mill."

"I don't think so. He's probably halfway to Texas by now, or somewhere equally remote."

"How many more interesting men are you keeping to yourself?" Ginnie asked, a mischievous twinkle in her eye.

"Oh, dozens. Actually, I don't even know whether he's married or not."

"You don't?"

"It didn't seem important. I never expected to see him again after he drove me into New Mill Friday. It was just the wildest coincidence I happened to see the news story about his accident and called the hospital to see if it could possibly be him. The operator connected me by mistake, and. . ."

Ginnie was hanging on every word as though it were some sort of lascivious gossip.

"Well, never mind. I don't ever expect to see Greg McCormick again."

"What a shame," Ginnie said with a sigh. "Not for you, of course," she added quickly, "but I wouldn't mind getting to know him."

"Oh, be sensible, Ginnie. He's just a truck driver. You need someone with a college degree. Someone who will have more in common with you."

"I know, but I can dream, can't I?"

"I'll give Sam a nudge. I'm sure he must have some friend who would be suitable for you."

"I don't want someone stuffy," Ginnie said, then chuckled. "On the other hand, I guess I'd better be realistic. Stuffy is better than nothing."

"Yes, Stanville is such a small town. It's a shame we don't have a better crop of eligible bachelors."

Ginnie changed the subject. "Do you think Sam is going to have a fit when you tell him you're postponing the wedding until June?"

"I'm afraid so. I'm dreading this. He put the pressure on me once, though, and I'm determined not to let it happen again."

They were approaching the edge of town. A line of fast-food restaurants and motels led into the outskirts. Ginnie turned off the highway onto the road leading to the downtown business district. "I'd like to go in and freshen up and have a Coke before I go back," she said.

"Why don't you stay and have dinner with us? I know Sam will insist."

"I'd better not tonight. You'll have plenty to talk about without me." She pulled into the parking lot adjacent to Sam's office building, and they both climbed out and went in.

As usual, Sam had someone in his office, and his secretary had gone home, so Chelsea sat down in his waiting room and picked up a magazine. Ginnie returned from the lounge and sat with her, finishing her Coke.

"Does he always work this late?" Ginnie asked in a low voice.

"Frequently. I think they need more accountants in this town. He's taken on far more than he can handle comfortably."

"Well, at least he's probably making lots of money."

"I'm sure he does well, but he's not what you'd call a big spender. I don't mean he's tight or anything, but he lives modestly."

They were still chatting when the door opened and a paunchy, middle-aged man took his leave of Sam and hurried out.

Sam smiled at the sight of them and came over and greeted Chelsea with a light kiss. He took Ginnie's hand and thanked her for driving Chelsea over. "You'll have dinner with us, won't you?"

"Not tonight, Sam. I need to get back, but I'll take a rain check." She tossed her paper cup in the wastebasket and turned to Chelsea. "See you later."

"Okay. Thanks a lot. I'll call you about that dinner." Chelsea watched her friend leave, then she turned to Sam. "Are you ready to go eat?"

"Yes, I thought we'd go to Murray's Place. We can go by my house and pick up your car on the way back." At the door, he turned her toward him and kissed her warmly.

She returned his kiss. "All right. Murray's sounds fine." They walked out to his car, and he pulled out and turned onto the road leading to Murray's Place, a casual little restaurant with a country atmosphere.

"Well, we're all set," he said cheerfully. "I picked up your blood test at noon, so that crisis is taken care of." He seemed pleased with the world as he went on. "The weather report sounds great for the weekend. Gradually warming temperatures and sunny. Typical spring weather."

She hated to bring him down. How should she start? "I guess that was the last storm of the season. I hope you weren't too terribly disappointed."

"You're absolutely right I was disappointed. How do you think I felt? I just hope your weekend wasn't too dreary. I know you must have been crushed, too." He reached over and patted her knee. "Well, we'll just have to look on the bright side. By being in the office during the storm, I managed to pick up a new client."

"You did?"

"Yes, that was him, Bertram McCoy. He owns the biggest grain elevator in this part of the country. Just called in, said he'd heard of me. Seemed impressed that I was working on the weekend. It's a big account."

She stared at him curiously. "Is that what you want, Sam? It seems to me you already have more business than you can handle, and now you're taking on another big account."

He pulled the car up to Murray's parking lot, and they went in. They were ushered to a table next to the window, where they ordered one of Murray's famous barbecue dinners.

Sam ignored the fact that she had reservations about his taking on more business. Somehow, it didn't seem important to him. Now, he was back on the subject of the wedding. "What do you think? Will everyone be able to go on with the plans this weekend?"

"I don't know. It seems like that's rushing things, isn't it?"

He looked crestfallen. "What do you mean? There's no reason not to, is there?"

"I. . .well, Sam, I've been thinking. You know I really would like to have a nice wedding, with all my friends, and my relatives from out of town."

He groaned and put his hands on his face in a gesture of futility.

Chelsea watched his expression carefully. This was the hard part, she knew.

"I thought we had all that settled," he said, frowning. A crease marred his handsome face.

"I know, and I hate to disappoint you, but this past week was so hectic, I just can't go through another like that."

Sam was silent, thinking this over. The waiter brought their drinks, and Sam took a deep swig of his Pepsi. "Everything's done now," he said. "A few telephone calls, and it's all set. What's the problem, Chelsea?"

"I only expect to get married once, and I want it to be done right. I'm sure you can understand how I feel."

Sam was looking more upset by the minute. "You do love me, don't you?"

"Oh, come on. You know I do. It isn't that at all. Now don't give me a bad time, dear."

"Just when were you thinking of having this elaborate wedding?"

"When school is out. In June. It's only two more months."

"That's too late." Sam's face was bereft of expression. He seemed to be making some inner calculation. The waiter brought their food, and this momentarily sidetracked the conversation.

As she ate, Chelsea glanced at Sam, wondering what he was really thinking.

He picked at his food, and finally pushed it aside. "I'm not hungry."

Chelsea wasn't enjoying her meal, either. "Perhaps we should go. I have some papers to grade before I go to bed."

"Yes," he said, motioning for the check. A pall had been cast over the evening, and Chelsea realized nothing she could say would change it, at least for this particular evening.

Sam took the check and fished his money out of his wallet, then they returned to his car. "I'll drop you off at your car," he said, and there was little more conversation as they drove back.

Once they reached his apartment, he walked her over to her car, parked in the driveway. He hadn't urged her to come in. He opened the car door for her, and she settled herself behind the wheel.

She rolled the car window down, and he gave her a perfunctory kiss before she backed out and started back to Stanville with a heavy heart.

One thought stayed with her all the way. *Am I losing him?*

four

"Yes, Mother, I know Sam was disappointed, but I think this is for the best. It's just a few short weeks." Chelsea tried to keep the irritation from her voice.

"I'd love to see you have a nice traditional wedding with all the trimmings, dear. You know that, but you're taking a big chance by being so independent with Sam. You could very well lose him, and let's face it, you're not getting any younger."

"Oh!" This was too much. "I'm not senile yet, and Sam isn't the only man in the world." *When did twenty-nine get to be so old?* she wondered.

"Yes, but he's ideal husband material, and men like that are scarce. You would be set for life with a decent man who makes an excellent income. Mark my words, Chelsea, you could do worse."

After they finished talking, Chelsea paced the floor in frustration. Not that she was surprised. Her mother had always insisted she should be on the lookout for a husband, and to her Sam was "Mr. Perfect." *She's probably anxious for a grandchild,* Chelsea decided.

Even Ginnie had seemed doubtful when Chelsea told her she was postponing the wedding. The only person who seemed to approve was Greg McCormick. Now Chelsea wished devoutly that she could talk to him.

Of course, she couldn't call him. He was probably on the road somewhere. She closed her eyes, concentrating on his face, bringing him closer in her imagination.

She had mentioned to her mother that she had added Aunt Joanne's name to her prayer circle. That had pleased her mother, who said Joanne was holding her own, but the chemo treatments were hard on her.

Just then the phone rang, startling her out of her reverie. Her heart pounded as she lifted the receiver.

It was Sam, sounding contrite. "I guess I didn't take the news of the postponement very well. I was just so disappointed." He wanted to see her Friday, have dinner, and talk over their plans. "And," he added, "I could try to make up for acting so badly."

Thursday and Friday inched by, dragging like the most boring lecture she had ever sat through. If it hadn't been for Jimmy Preston, Chelsea feared she might actually have died of boredom; however, Jimmy didn't let her down.

On Thursday he sat in the cafeteria at noon, eating a piece of fried chicken. He and Tommy Adams were clowning around. All of a sudden Jimmy gasped, and his eyes bugged out. Tommy ran to Mr. Culpepper and told him something was wrong with Jimmy.

By the time Mr. Culpepper could get to him, Jimmy was turning blue. Mr. Culpepper did a Heimlich maneuver on him, and a chicken bone, which had been caught in his throat, popped out.

The children had been standing around, staring with horror at what was happening. When they saw that Jimmy was going to be all right, they cheered and became rowdier than Chelsea had ever seen them. She looked at Jean Sims, who was monitoring the lunch hour with her, and Jean just shook her head and shrugged. She was right, of course. Let them get it out of their systems before they returned to class.

She looked around for Mr. Culpepper, wanting to compliment him on his quick action in saving the Preston boy, but he had left. "Did you see Mr. Culpepper leave?" she asked Jean.

"Yes, he went out to the teacher's lounge, looking rather green."

"Mmm, maybe I'd better check on him. Can you keep an eye on things here for a few minutes?"

"Sure, but don't stay long. These wild hyenas might take over the school."

"I won't be long," Chelsea promised.

She found Mr. Culpepper lying down, looking shaken. "Are you all right?"

He sat up, doing his best to appear normal. "Yes, I was just resting." He smoothed his hair with a shaking hand.

"That was awfully impressive the way you saved Jimmy Preston. It happened before Jean and I knew anything was wrong."

"Yes, these things can happen in a split second, and a child can lose his life before anyone is aware he was in trouble. We were lucky this time."

Chelsea didn't like Mr. Culpepper's color. "Why don't you rest a while longer, sir, and I'll get you something to drink. How about a glass of orange juice?"

"Yes, Chelsea, that should snap me out of it."

She hurried to the cafeteria to fetch the juice, and at the same time to reassure Jean that she would be right back.

Mr. Culpepper was sitting up when she returned, still rather limp and pale-looking.

"This will fix you up," Chelsea said, handing him the juice. *He looks old,* she observed. *He must be nearing retirement age.*

As she turned to go, he assured her he would be back in his office in a few minutes. She never thought she would feel such concern for the principal, with his dignified, rather forbidding air. He had been somewhat intimidating, but now she saw him in a different light. He entered her thoughts more than once the rest of the day.

Friday was another dull day. She had never been bored with teaching before. *I probably need a change,* she decided.

As soon as class took up after recess, Chelsea turned around from writing the assignment on the board, and noticed Jimmy Preston's seat was empty. She sighed. What now?

The class was half over when Jimmy returned in triumph, grinning and holding up a bandaged finger. There were nudges and whispers all over the room as the children tried to find out what had happened to their friend.

No doubt about it, Chelsea thought, *I've lost them.* She tapped on her desk to get their attention. "Quiet, please." Once she could be heard, she continued. "Jimmy, will you please explain to us what happened to make you late returning to class?"

Jimmy stood up, looking ever so pleased with himself, and held up his bandaged finger. "Sorry to be late, Miss Morgan. I was stung by a bee out on the playground."

"I'm sorry to hear that, Jimmy. I hope it's better now."

"Yes, ma'am. I went into the nurse's office and she pulled the stinger out. She put some medicine on it, and it still hurt, so she bandaged it up."

"So it's all right now."

Funny how a bandage can make things better for a kid, she thought.

"Now that we all know what happened to Jimmy, we can get back to discussing the assignment."

The school bell finally rang, and Chelsea cleared her desk for the weekend and went home.

She pulled first one dress, then another, out of the closet, trying to decide which one to wear on her date with Sam.

Not that it mattered. She finally went eeny-meeny-miny-mo and chose the blue one. Sam had seen it dozens of times, but it was becoming.

On the drive over to New Mill, she turned the radio up loud, getting in the mood for her date. *Actually,* she told herself, *it's one of the most beautiful spring days I've ever seen.* Still chilly, but sunny and breezy, with white clouds scudding along in a bright blue sky.

Wasn't this about the place where her car had broken down that fateful night? There was a faint smile on her face. She couldn't help thinking of Greg McCormick. What a guy! Where was he now? Probably driving his big semi clear across the country, his radio turned on to a Western music station, without a care in the world.

She sighed dreamily. What she wouldn't give to be meeting him all over again today.

Be realistic, she told herself. *He probably hasn't given you a thought since he last saw you.*

As much as she hated to admit it, her mother was probably right. If she wasn't careful, Sam would slip away, and she would wish she had him back.

Dusk was falling over the little town when she finally pulled her car into the parking space in front of Sam's office. She took a deep breath and went inside. Dolores would be gone by now, and he should be waiting and ready to go.

From long experience, Chelsea knew this was wishful thinking. She tapped on his office door and called out, "I'm here, Sam."

"Be with you in a few minutes," he called. "Make yourself comfortable."

This meant he was with a client and no telling how long she would have to wait. She sat down and started leafing through an ancient magazine.

It seemed as if eons had passed while she alternately read and got up and went over to gaze out the window. Couldn't he ever be on time?

Suddenly, the door burst open, and she heard the low conversation of two masculine voices, congenial, like old friends. Sam preceded his client, and Chelsea looked up just as they came out of the dark hallway into the light.

Sam put his arm around her shoulders in a proprietary gesture. "Here she is, Greg. I want you to meet Chelsea Morgan, my fiancée."

"How do you do," Greg McCormick said, taking her hand. "Sam has told me a lot about you." He never changed expression.

Chelsea didn't do so well, though. Her voice broke disgustingly as she acknowledged his greeting, and heaven knows what her expression must have shown.

Fortunately, Sam didn't notice. He hadn't looked at her, being so intent on impressing his client with his good fortune.

"I had better run," Greg said. "It was nice meeting you, Miss. . ." he hesitated, "Miss Morgan."

Sam showed him to the door, then returned to Chelsea.

"That was Greg McCormick," he said proudly. "He's a new client. Owns a big trucking company."

There was a momentary silence. "Owns? Did you say *owns?*"

"Yes," Sam replied enthusiastically. "His trucking line is one of the most profitable in this part of the country. I don't mind telling you, I'm mighty pleased to have him as a client. He's one of the best accounts I've secured in a long time."

Chelsea sat there like a statue, staring off into space, while all this registered. Somehow, she just couldn't come up with the right words to match Sam's enthusiasm.

"That's fine, Sam. I'm glad," she said weakly.

"Well, let's go eat," he said, turning toward the door. "I'm starved." He stopped at the door and turned around, giving her an adoring look and a smile, then he leaned down and kissed her.

She had been annoyed that he kept her waiting, but that was easy enough to forgive, she reasoned. She squeezed his arm affectionately. She had to stop behaving like such a pill. Sam was a good man, and he deserved better.

As they drove, she was silent, rehashing the scene in Sam's office. Why had she and Greg carried on that ridiculous charade, pretending they had never met before? It was almost like lying.

"You know, Sam, there's something I've been wanting us to talk about."

"What's that, honey?"

"Well, you know how I feel about my faith. I hope you feel the same way. I wish we'd talk about it more. It's important to me."

"Sure, dear. What do you want to know?"

"I couldn't help noticing you skip church during tax season, and I don't think you've ever taken me to any of the activities you have at your church."

"I know. It's a shame that everything is so crowded into that short tax season. I have to make some sacrifices. I'm sure you can understand that."

"Don't you miss it? My father was a busy small-town lawyer, but I don't remember that he was ever too busy to take his family to church."

"Well, those were different times."

"I'm sure you must have a lot of friends in your church. Attending some of their little suppers would give me an opportunity to meet some of them."

"Yes, well, I'll see what I can do about that."

Sam turned his car in at the Pines, and Glenn greeted them

enthusiastically. "I've been wondering when you folks would be getting back here." He smiled broadly. "I missed seeing you last weekend."

He ushered them to a table and handed them a couple of menus. "Your waiter will be right with you. Enjoy your meal."

As usual, they both read through the entire menu, which hadn't been changed in the last five years.

"What are you going to have?" Chelsea asked.

"I don't know," Sam replied. "I had the steak last time." He continued perusing the menu. "What are you going to have?"

"I don't know. Do you suppose the lasagna is any good?"

"I couldn't say. I don't like all that Italian stuff. I'm strictly a meat-and-potatoes kind of guy."

The waiter appeared, and he was the first new thing they had seen at the Pines since they had been eating there. "I'm Thurman, and I'll be your waiter. Can I get you folks something to drink?"

"Just iced tea," Chelsea said.

Sam said he'd just have tea, too.

Once the preliminaries were over, Chelsea knew the conversation would return to the postponed wedding date. She mentally prepared herself. It was hard to understand why Sam was so adamant about postponing the date. They were only talking about a few weeks. In fact, less than two months, and the time would go by fast.

Thurman was back with their tea. "Now," he said, "what can I bring you for dinner?"

Chelsea spoke first. "I'll have the lasagna."

Sam ordered the roast beef.

It was a low-key, comfortable sort of place, and they were perfectly at ease. *Almost like an old married couple already,* she mused, glancing at Sam.

Now he looked up, once more in an exuberant mood.

Smiling, he lifted his glass. "Here's to my new client."

Chelsea echoed his gesture. "To Greg McCormick," and sipped the cold, refreshing tea.

They talked of her latest letter from her mother, and of course, Sam continued to press for an immediate wedding, insisting he loved her enough to overlook the problems of going ahead now.

"Don't forget, Sam, next Sunday is Easter. We know we can't get married that weekend, and we need to make our plans. Where would you rather attend Easter services, here or in Stanville?"

"Oh, I had completely forgotten. It kind of sneaked up on me, what with everything else that has been going on. I guess it would be best to go here, then we can go on to the party on the grounds of the Van Oghden estate."

This had been a tradition as far back as Chelsea could remember. There was an Easter egg hunt for the children and a barbecue set out under a big tent. "I thought maybe they wouldn't have it this year, since Mr. Oghden died last November."

"I understand he provided for it to be continued in his will."

"What a nice gesture."

Sam nodded, and tried to return the conversation to the wedding date, but the waiter interrupted with the arrival of their food.

Once the food was served and the waiter was gone, Chelsea looked up at Sam with a smile. "You know, dear, I almost feel guilty that we have these times together, and a future to look forward to, and Ginnie doesn't have anything but work."

"Yes, it does seem a shame. I'll give it some thought."

"Oh, would you, Sam? That would be wonderful. We could double-date."

"I kind of thought we didn't need anyone," Sam said, looking hurt.

"Maybe we don't, but she does," Chelsea said.

The lasagna wasn't as good as what Chelsea could make at home, but it was okay. She noticed Sam seemed to enjoy his roast beef. He ate it very rare

"Did you enjoy your dinner?" Sam asked as they finished their food.

"Yes, it was fine. Did you?"

"Yeah, it was just great. Their food is always dependable. How about some dessert?"

"Not tonight. I couldn't eat another bite."

"Okay." He caught Thurman's eye and asked for the check. "We can have some coffee at home," he said.

There wasn't much conversation as they drove back to Sam's house. He turned the radio up, and the music from the easy-listening station took over.

As usual, once they were back at his apartment, Chelsea volunteered to make the coffee. Sam had made it the first time she had come in with him after dinner, and it had been horrible. Now, she always made it, and he seemed to appreciate it.

"You know, Chelsea," he said, taking a sip as they sat in his living room, "you make the best coffee of anyone I know."

"Thanks, Sam," she said, settling back comfortably.

He reached out and pulled her over next to him. "Don't sit so far away."

She moved next to him and snuggled into the bend of his arm. He hugged her tight. "That's more like it," he said, patting her shoulder affectionately.

He waited for her to take a sip of the coffee and set down her cup on the table, then he gave her a long kiss.

She stiffened. What was the matter with her? Suddenly she didn't even want to kiss him.

Finally, he released her. "Now, doesn't that make you want to get married right away?"

"Uh, well, I still think it would be better to wait." She took another sip of her coffee.

He looked into her face with concern. "Is something wrong?"

"It's nothing, Sam. I just have a little headache. It must have been something I ate."

"Maybe there were sulfates in the salad."

"You may be right. I hate to spoil the evening, but I really think I should go. It's a long drive home, and besides, I know you need to get up early in the morning. There must be a lot of work involved in setting up your new client's account."

"You're right about that. I'll have to get an early start. In fact, I plan to work right through the weekend."

"Well, I'll just run along and let you get some rest."

"Are you sure you feel up to the drive?"

"Yes, I'll be all right. A good night's sleep should fix me up."

He walked her out to the car. "I'll think about your suggestion and see if I can come up with someone for Ginnie."

"I'd appreciate that, Sam."

He opened her car door, and she lowered the window.

"You know, that new client of mine would be an ideal match for her, except. . ." He didn't finish.

"Except what?"

"Oh, nothing. Never mind." He leaned over and kissed her. "Good night. I'll call." He turned and went back to the house as she backed out, a puzzled expression on her face.

five

Another week passed uneventfully, and Sam had called asking for a date on Friday. At least, he was driving to Stanville for a change.

Chelsea didn't like to drive over to New Mill all the time, even though it did give him an extra hour to work. That was why she had decided to transfer her job to the New Mill school when they were married.

She planned ahead to have the hem done on her new spring outfit so she could wear it on her date. By Friday, she was feeling more like old times. She was looking forward to going out with Sam, hoping things would be as they were when they first met.

After school, she hurried home and straightened up the living room. There wasn't much in the mail except for a note from her cousin Louise in Chicago. She read it hastily and set it aside. Louise had just heard Chelsea had postponed her wedding because of the snowstorm, and was sorry.

She went into her bedroom and took out her clothes for that night. Her mood steadily improved as she stood under the shower.

She had just stepped out and started to dry off, when the telephone rang. She wrapped the towel around her and padded into the bedroom to answer it.

Sam was on the other end of the line, sounding very contrite. "I hate to call you so late like this, dear, but something has come up."

Chelsea waited, hoping he hadn't had a heart attack or a

52 The Reluctant Bride

death in the family.

"A rush job," he explained. "Has to be out by tomorrow." He did sound unhappy.

"Then you won't be able to come over at all?" She couldn't keep the disappointment from her voice.

"I'm sure you understand, dear. It's going to be good for our future, you know. We have to think of it that way. An important client. I just couldn't say no. You do understand, don't you?"

"Yes, I suppose so."

"I'll call you tomorrow. We'll see how it goes. Maybe I can spare some time tomorrow night."

"All right, Sam. Good-bye."

"Good-bye, dear. Love you."

Chelsea replaced the receiver, and her gaze fell on her new outfit lying on the bed. She sighed audibly. Why did Sam always have to put his work first?

She hung the new clothes back in the closet, and pulled out her oldest, grungiest pair of jeans and an old purple sweatshirt with a hole in the sleeve. It just seemed to match her rapidly deteriorating mood. She paced the floor a while, trying to dispel some of her disappointment.

That settles it, she mused, *I'm definitely postponing the wedding.*

She settled down to read her new library book, reminding herself she wasn't any worse off than Ginnie or any of a number of her unmarried friends. There were worse things than an evening spent with a good book.

She had been reading about half an hour when it occurred to her she would have to fix herself something to eat tonight. She went to the kitchen and started poking around in the refrigerator. It didn't look too hopeful. *Perhaps some scrambled eggs,* she decided, without much enthusiasm.

She had pulled out her skillet and started to break the eggs, when the phone rang. It was probably Sam again. Perhaps he had thought better of canceling their date.

She crossed over to the phone and answered quietly. "Hello."

It certainly wasn't Sam.

"This is Greg McCormick."

"Oh, Greg. Hello." Things were looking up.

"I had to be in town for some business. I know it's awfully late to call, but I was wondering if you could have dinner with me tonight."

"I'd love to. I'm glad you called when you did. I was just getting ready to fix something."

"Good. I'll be by in about twenty minutes."

Chelsea replaced the telephone receiver and turned into a whirling dervish. She slammed the skillet into the cabinet, ran to her bedroom and yanked off her old jeans and the grungy purple sweatshirt. She kicked them into the closet, and lovingly pulled her new outfit over her head.

Thank You, Lord. For a while there she had forgotten her favorite Bible verse, Romans 8:28: "All things work together for good to them that love God."

Next, she ran to the bathroom and started working on her hair, which refused to cooperate. "Come on!" she muttered. "This is an emergency. Get with it." She finally prevailed over it, then she went to work on her makeup.

She had just finished the process and stepped back to admire the results when she heard her doorbell. She took a deep breath and, with great dignity, slowly walked into the living room and opened the door.

"Hi!" Greg said, and he had that kind of lopsided grin that drove her crazy.

"Hello," she said, and invited him in. "I hadn't expected to hear from you." She motioned for him to sit on the sofa.

"Make yourself comfortable. Could I get you something before we go?"

"No, thanks. I'll just wait until we get to the restaurant." He looked her over admiringly. "Nice outfit."

"Thanks. I'll get my purse, and we can be off." That's when she remembered that long, first step to the truck cab. She glanced down at her skirt. Had she made a mistake? It might be too tight.

He rose when she returned and held the front door for her. Once outside, she looked around for his big semi, but it was nowhere in sight. He led the way to a nice late-model car and unlocked the door.

"Here we are," he said, as she climbed in. He closed the door and went around to his side and slid in under the wheel.

She laughed. "I had a bad moment when we started out. I was expecting your semi, and I knew my skirt was so tight I wouldn't be able to manage that first step."

He chuckled. "I do drive a car occasionally." Then he became more serious. "Look, I hope you don't mind my calling you on the spur of the moment like this."

"Not at all. I had plans, but something came up, so it all worked out fine. Where are we going?"

"I thought we'd go to Barcarolle if that's all right with you. It has a nice, soothing atmosphere at night."

"Good. It's my favorite."

Inside, nearly every table was occupied. A votive candle on each table emitted a rosy glow, and there was a pleasant hum of conversation in the background.

Greg gave the hostess his name, and she ushered them to a quiet table in the corner. They ordered, and Chelsea noticed Greg was looking unusually self-satisfied. She supposed he hadn't really expected her to go out with him.

He started to say something, but waited until the waitress

had brought them ice water and departed. Then he looked up. "So, when's the wedding now? I believe you said you were postponing it."

"Not until June. I wanted to wait until school was out."

"Good idea. I guess old what's-his-name didn't like that too well."

"Sam? No, he wasn't pleased, but I think it will be for the best." She took a sip of her ice water. This wasn't a matter she wanted to discuss tonight. She decided to change the subject. "When will you be going on one of your cross-country drives in your semi?"

"Whenever one of my drivers can't make his run. That could be anytime. I'm always ready." Now he gave her a penetrating look. "How come you're not out with. . .uh, Sam. . .tonight?"

So he's back to that again, she thought. "Oh, we had plans but he had to cancel at the last minute. He had to get out some work for an important client. . ."

Suddenly she stopped and stared at Greg. *Oh, no! He wouldn't do a thing like that. Would he?*

There was a twinkle in his eye, and that self-satisfied look was still there.

A wave of anger swept her. "You did this! How could you?"

"Oh, then you mean he canceled because of that little job I gave him? I had no idea he'd do that. I am sorry."

He did sound sincere, but she had her doubts. What if he had planned it that way, deliberately interfered in her life? She shot him an angry glance. He seemed utterly complacent. Chelsea tried to calm her inner seething.

"Sam takes his work very seriously, in case you didn't know it. It's one of his good qualities. If you give him a job to do, he always gets it out on time, no matter what."

"No matter what," he repeated. "I guess that's a good quality, sometimes, but then you know him better than I do." Greg gulped down part of his water. "I'm glad it worked out the way it did anyway. Why don't we relax and enjoy the rest of the evening, since we're here."

"All right." There was a bit of a pout in her voice. "This is a nice place, and there's nothing to be gained by dwelling on poor Sam back at his office slaving away."

The waitress refilled their water glasses, and Greg took another drink. "I'm still congratulating myself for finding you free this evening," he said, giving her a warm smile.

Some of the anger began to drain out of her as she realized how sincere he was.

"We do need to have a chance to know each other better," he said. "After all, when I picked you up on the highway that day, looking like a lost orphan, we were perfect strangers. Then, the next time I saw you, I had a concussion and wasn't in shape to turn on my legendary charm." He grinned at this exaggeration.

"Legendary charm?" she mocked. "Will I be able to resist?" But he was hard to resist. She took a deep breath.

"What do you say? Can't we be friends?"

"All right, but I don't want Sam to know about this. Not yet."

The waitress brought their food. They had ordered the veal parmigiana, and the aroma was mouth-watering.

Chelsea was already feeling better. After all, she realized, it was Sam she should be mad at, not Greg. In fact, it was awfully hard to be mad at Greg.

She stole a glance at him. Ginnie was right. He was the most attractive man she had ever seen. His hair had been carefully combed tonight, but it still managed to fall over his forehead in little clumps. His grin warmed her all over, and when he looked at her with that serious expression in his eyes, it made her feel all shivery.

"You're right," she said. "We should get to know each

other better. Tell me about your family."

He hesitated, as though he didn't know where to start. "My family," he repeated. "Well, there's my mother, a nice traditional lady who was always at home, usually in the kitchen, making life comfortable for my father and her boys. She's kind of short and plump and pleasant-looking. I get my height from my father's side of the family."

Chelsea prodded him to continue. "And what about the rest of your family?"

"My dad is about the swellest guy in the world. He's tough, and a good businessman, but he would do anything for his family. Life hasn't been easy for him." He stopped, and his eyes took on a faraway expression.

"Did you appreciate him when you were growing up, or did that come later?"

"I think not until I was grown and knew a little something about life. He was a tough, demanding father, and he kept us in line." He shrugged. "I guess it was for the best. Otherwise, I might have become a spoiled brat, since spoiling us was what my mother did best."

"What about your brother? Was there just one?"

"Yeah, Clint. He's three years older." Once more, there was that faraway look. "Now, tell me about your family."

"No more about your brother?"

"I'll show you his picture sometime. Now it's your turn."

"Well, I'm afraid my mother was just the opposite of yours. Oh, she was traditional, at least in her beliefs, but she worked. She was a teacher and later on a guidance counselor. She thought teaching was the only profession suitable for a woman."

"So that's why you took up teaching?"

"Partly. Mother took her work very seriously, and so do I. On the other hand, I'll have to admit I envied my friends whose mothers were home all the time. It wasn't much fun coming home to an empty house after school, because she frequently had meetings."

"It sounds like she was ahead of her time."

"Yes, that about says it all." Chelsea tasted her food. . . perfect. "It must have been a pleasant childhood for you. Where did you grow up?"

"In Chicago. My family still lives there." Greg took a big bite of his veal parmigiana, and savoured it. "My mother used to make this. They do it well here."

"Yes, it is good." Chelsea sipped her water, glancing up at Greg through her lashes as she did. A warm feeling of well-being went through her. "It must have been exciting growing up in Chicago. I grew up in a tiny little town in Illinois, Bedford, population 4,000."

Greg smiled at her in a very special way, somehow excluding the rest of the world. "Small-town girls are the best."

"It didn't seem so at the time. I thought it was terribly boring. I had to grow up to appreciate it."

"I certainly wouldn't want to raise my children in Chicago," he said. "It is a very dangerous place in more ways than one."

"I'm sure you're right. Tell me, are your parents still living?"

"Yes, and in good health."

"My father died when I was sixteen. I'll never forget the feeling of losing him. I simply adored him. He lived for my mother and me, and we had that special feeling of knowing he put us first."

"So, you're an only child, eh?"

"Yes, and don't give me that old cliché about being a spoiled only child. It just isn't true."

His eyebrows raised at her remark. "You're awfully defensive, aren't you?"

"I suppose so. It's just that I get tired of hearing that."

They were silent for a while, then she couldn't suppress her curiosity any longer. "Have you ever been married?"

If he were surprised by her directness, he didn't show it. He just chuckled good-naturedly. "No. I'm one of those nimble bachelors who somehow manages to avoid the big capitulation."

I'll bet, she thought. "Have you ever come close?"

"Not as close as you," he answered.

"I had that coming. It serves me right for being so nosy."

"Is your conscience bothering you? An engaged woman being out with another man?"

She thought about that for a moment. "Not really, but I suppose it should."

"Maybe that's because you're not quite sure," he suggested.

She sighed. She didn't want to think of that tonight. "I'll have to give that some thought later. Not about getting married, just about postponing it. Sam isn't a bad person, you know. He has a lot of good attributes you probably wouldn't appreciate."

"Oh, is that so?" His raised eyebrow called for a further explanation.

"I just meant he's a very decent, hardworking person who makes a good living and who loves me and is ready to marry me the minute I say the word."

"Yes, but I think the question is, are you ready to marry him on a moment's notice? I think I know the answer to that."

"You have a way of making me feel very uncomfortable, Greg. I wish you wouldn't talk like this."

"Sorry." He drained his water glass. "How about some dessert and coffee?"

"Why don't we go back to my place for some coffee and cookies?"

"Fine. I'd like that." He motioned for the waiter and asked for the check.

Outside in the car, she turned to him. "That was a delicious meal. I really enjoyed it."

"So did I, but I enjoyed the company more."

It was a perfect evening, not warm, but not uncomfortably cold. There was the smell of spring in the air, all fresh and earthy and fragrant.

He glanced her way. "What are you thinking?"

"I'm getting used to the idea of you driving a regular car instead of a big semi. There's something so macho and exciting about a man who herds one of those monsters around the country."

He laughed. "I kind of like that. Do you really think of me as macho and exciting?" He tuned in some Western music, and sat back, looking terribly pleased with himself.

She longed to think of something to say to burst that self-satisfied bubble, but no inspiration came. "I shouldn't have said that," she admitted. "Now you'll have to live up to that image, and I don't know how much of that I can stand."

"I'll try not to be a pain in the neck." He pulled his car into a space in front of her apartment building and turned off the motor. Coming around to her side, he opened her door.

She felt his hand under her elbow as they climbed the steps up to the entrance. As she unlocked the door, she heard the telephone ringing. She hurried to answer it, with Greg following.

It was Sam, sounding lonely. "I'm going to be through in about an hour. I don't suppose I could come over so late, could I?"

She hesitated, momentarily at a loss, then looked over at Greg, waiting patiently, knowing of course who was on the line.

"Chelsea, are you there?"

"Yes, Sam. I'm sorry. By the time you drove over here, it would be so late. I'm really kind of tired tonight. Maybe we should postpone it."

"You're probably right, hon. It's just that I miss you. Tomorrow night then?"

"Okay."

"I'll pick you up at seven, and we'll have dinner. I love you."

"Yes, all right. Good-bye." She hadn't been able to say the words with Greg listening. What kind of person was she? Now she was seeing another man and deceiving her fiancé. She sighed. *This has got to stop,* she told herself as she replaced the receiver.

"Problems?" Greg asked, as she filled the coffeepot.

"Not really. That was Sam. He's through with his work and he wanted to come over. I think he knew before he called me it was too late, but he wanted to see me."

"That's understandable. I take it you're not going to tell him about us."

She looked up from measuring the coffee. "Us? You mean going to dinner?"

"I mean the whole thing, dinner, our friendship, the whole bit."

"Oh, I don't think so. It would be rather awkward, don't you think?"

He shrugged. "Maybe. We did fall into the subterfuge of pretending we were meeting for the first time in Sam's office, didn't we?"

"Yes. That was a mistake, but it can't be undone." She poured the coffee, and they carried their cups into the living room. "Let's not talk about it."

He seemed to be assessing her mood as he drank his coffee.

"You're not letting this bother you too much, are you?"

"No, of course not. I'll find some way to tell Sam, and we'll go on as before." She reached over and handed him the plate of cookies she had arranged earlier on the coffee table. "Have a cookie."

He had that questioning look as he observed her. She tried to ignore it, but finally her curiosity made her ask, "What are you thinking about?"

"I'm still trying to figure you out. Are you as cool as you seem? Or is all this juggling of dates getting under your skin?"

She laughed nervously. "What do you think?"

He was quiet for a moment, watching her expression raptly. "I'll tell you what I think, Chelsea. I think you're a very nice person who finds herself in a very uncomfortable position. I must say, though, you're carrying it off quite well."

"Well, thanks, I think." Of course, he was right, but she wasn't about to let him know. "At least you think I'm a nice person. As for being uncomfortable, actually I don't think there's anything to be bothered about."

He chuckled. "Maybe not, but I have my doubts. The evening isn't over yet."

Another veiled remark. Had she been mistaken inviting him in? "I think it's possible for a woman to have male friends as well as female friends, don't you?"

"It should be, although I've heard it argued that friendship between the sexes is impossible, because sex always gets in the way."

"That's ridiculous. Anyway, in my case it would be. After all, I'm engaged to another man, and I have no reason to believe you're not a perfect gentleman."

The beginnings of a smile twitched on his lips. "I've been called everything else at various times. Now I have something new to live up to."

"Really." She nibbled on a cookie. "I still don't know much about you. What are your hobbies, for instance? No. Let me guess. You love football and maybe baseball. You like to bowl. And I'll bet you like horses."

He was laughing now, holding his head back and laughing out loud. "You think you have me pegged, don't you? A real blue-collar lout. I like sports, sure, although bowling is something I can take or leave. I prefer golf and tennis, I like to cook, and believe it or not, I love an evening at the symphony."

"You're kidding. But you always turn on Western music when you're driving."

"Yeah, I know. It seems to fit the circumstances, especially when I'm driving a semi. There isn't much good music on the radio, and I like to choose my own. Oh, I have a few favorite tapes I play in the car, but out on the open road, the Western music seems just right."

"What about horses? Surely I was right about something."

"Horses?" He laughed again. "Just because I like Western music, does it follow I have to love horses? Actually, I've never been on one."

"Well, I'll bet if you tried to guess what I like you'd be as far off as I was."

"Okay. I'll take that challenge, but first heat up my coffee a bit."

She went to the kitchen and brought the coffeepot in, poured some into his cup, and set the pot on the table. "All right." She settled back on the sofa. "What are my favorite hobbies?"

He regarded her steadily for a moment, then answered. "You like decorating, and gardening, and reading; furthermore, I suspect you're a bit of an artist."

"That's very good," she said admiringly. "How did you come so close? You're absolutely right, except that I'm not much of an artist. More of a dabbler."

"It was easy. Anyone can tell you're a good decorator just by looking at your apartment. I had to assume it wasn't professionally decorated. I see plants and flowers around everywhere, and I don't think Sam's the kind to send them. As for the art, you just seem like an artistic sort of person."

"I'd love to paint more, but there just isn't time."

"As for the reading," he said, "you're kind of quiet and introspective, like a person who enjoys reading."

"Right again. I particularly like English novels."

He nodded. "It figures. I read a lot of history and adventure when I'm on the road."

She gave him a long, searching look. Could they really be friends, or should she end it tonight? Was she being unfair to Sam? "You know, Greg, I'm glad we had this little evening together. I hope I'm not wrong in thinking we can be friends. I mean, without hurting Sam. You think so, too, don't you?"

"Well yes and no. In the context of my religion, I'd have to say it's questionable."

"Tell me about your religion. I don't think we've ever discussed that. Are you a Christian?"

"Yes, of course. I'm an active church member. I attend every Sunday, support their fund-raisers, and in general make it a big part of my life. How about you?"

"I feel the same way. It's the most important part of my life."

Greg gave her an approving nod. "And I suppose Sam feels the same way?"

Chelsea was quiet and thoughtful. Finally she spoke hesitantly. "I. . .wish I could be sure. He frequently works on Sunday instead of attending church."

Greg didn't comment. Finally he glanced at his watch. "It's getting late. I'd better go."

She followed him to the door. "I enjoyed the evening."

"So did I." He put his hands on her shoulders and looked deep into her eyes. "Is that what you really want, Chelsea? To be my friend?" He was close enough that she could almost feel his warmth through her clothes.

She took a deep breath, collecting her thoughts, but before she could answer, he drew her closer and his mouth met hers in a kiss so warm and firm no other answer was necessary.

six

Saturday night in Stanville was just about as busy as in any other small town. The high-schoolers were out in force in their cars, congregating in front of fast-food restaurants. The young singles, like Chelsea, were at Barcarolle, and the more stable older crowd was dining in coats and ties at Bramwell's Inn.

Since Chelsea had just dined at Barcarolle with Greg, she told Sam she would like to try something different. "I've never had dinner at Bramwell's Inn, have you?"

"No, why don't we give it a try?" Sam was anxious to please her, since he had disappointed her last night. "I just hope they can seat us, since we don't have reservations."

There was a bit of a wait, so they sat down on one of the benches inside the entrance. It was fun to watch the more sedate diners arrive, properly dressed, with early reservations. Chelsea recognized Ginnie's parents, who stopped to chat. They had never met Sam, but said they had heard a lot about him.

Eventually, they were seated, and Sam ordered his usual steak and baked potato. Chelsea reminded herself inwardly that she wouldn't have to worry about taking cooking lessons when they were married. She settled for a broiled salmon steak.

Sam was apologetic about canceling out on her last night. "That new client you met the other day came in with an order which he needed right away. I didn't feel like I could turn him down under the circumstances."

"I understand, Sam. Don't worry about it." She had guessed

right. Greg had pulled a fast one on them, and she resented it. Now, he was the last thing she wanted to think about. Unfortunately, with the thought of him came the sensation of his good-night kiss. . .not so easily forgotten.

". . .And I think we could move right after the honeymoon, don't you?" Sam was talking to her.

"I'm sorry, honey. What were you saying?"

"I was thinking ahead to our moving plans. You know, once we're married you'll have to move."

"Of course, but I think we'd better do a little house hunting, don't you?"

"You can move into my apartment until we're settled."

"Maybe we could build a new house."

"Perhaps, but I had something else in mind."

"Oh, well then, let's discuss it."

"Not tonight." The waiter brought their food, steaming hot and irresistible.

Chelsea didn't want to get involved in an argument right now. "We'll talk about it later. This food looks absolutely delicious. We should come here more often."

Sam nodded. "I take it we're going to the regular church service in the morning."

"Yes, it would be awfully early for me to have to get up and drive over in time for the early service. Anyway, you know I enjoy seeing what everyone is wearing. In my grandmother's day people always wore a brand-new outfit on Easter Sunday. That made it more festive."

"Yes. Now we're lucky if the men bother with coats and ties."

Sam didn't waste any time getting off on his favorite subject. "Now that you've had a little time to think about it, when do you want to have the wedding? How about next weekend?"

"Well, I have given it some serious thought, Sam, and I want to have it right after school is out, the first week in June." Her tone was very definite, and Sam blinked and stared at her.

He evaluated her for several long minutes. "That won't do, Chelsea. I may as well tell you, it has to be no later than May fourteenth."

"I'm sorry, Sam. Surely you can wait a few weeks longer."

"Well, no, I can't."

She responded to that with a little nervous laugh. "I can't believe you're serious."

He regarded her with a level gaze. "I do mean it, believe me. You won't be sorry, hon."

Chelsea took a sip of hot coffee, as she thought this over, she realized they had come to a serious impasse. She tried to lighten the situation. "I never heard of a couple breaking up because they couldn't agree on the wedding date."

Sam didn't even smile. "I wouldn't want us to be the first."

"Easter is very special to me. You know how I feel about that. Let's not spoil it this year. I'll pray about it. Maybe we should discuss it with the minister of your church. How about that?"

Sam shook his head. "It isn't up to him."

"Well, we don't have to make that decision this very minute. We'll talk about it later." This unexpected development gave Chelsea a headache, and she didn't want their evening together to be ruined.

After dinner, they went to Chelsea's apartment, where she turned on some music and offered him some cookies and coffee. She settled for half a cup. "I shouldn't have drunk so much at the restaurant." She sat close to Sam and munched a cookie.

He put his arm around her and sighed comfortably. "You

realize I love you, don't you?"

"Of course, and I love you, too." She was quiet for a moment. "You know, Sam, we've never talked about a lot of important things."

"Like what?"

"Like how many children do you want?"

"Oh, I never gave that much thought. I'm sure we can agree on whatever makes you happy. I'll just go along with you."

"And how do you feel about church? You know I'm pretty committed to being active in the church, and about attending regularly."

"Sure. That's okay with me."

"I never heard you say anything about God or prayer or any of your beliefs. You do believe in God, don't you?"

"Yeah, I guess so. No reason not to. I certainly don't object to your involvement in all that church stuff."

"Does that mean you won't be involved, too?"

"Well, I can't spend too much time on it. You know I have a heavy work schedule. I'll go as much as I can if that's what you want."

Chelsea pulled away and gave him a long look. "It seems to me that you are awfully agreeable to a lot of important things that affect our entire lives together, but you're downright inflexible about a minor matter such as our wedding date. I'm afraid I don't really understand you."

Sam rose and paced the floor. "So we're back to that. If you really loved me, Chelsea, and as you say, that's such a minor matter, then it seems to me you should go along with me on that."

Chelsea rose. "I'll give it some thought, hon. Now I think you had better go. I have a bit of a headache. I'll see you in the morning."

"Okay, dear." She saw him to the door, and he kissed her good night.

"Drive carefully," she admonished.

As she got ready for bed, Chelsea thought about their evening. There was only one conclusion that occurred to her. She was about to marry the most stubborn man in the world.

Dear Lord, she prayed, *please guide me in my relationship with Sam, and help me to make the right decision about whether to be adamant in my wish to postpone our marriage until June.*

❧

Easter morning Chelsea awoke to the sun streaming in the window. She could hear the birds singing outside, and she was filled with joy.

Thank You, Lord, for this glorious day.

As she showered and dressed, she made up her mind not to do anything to mar this special occasion. She would watch her words and stay off any touchy subjects. Surely she and Sam could find a compromise that would suit them both.

She had driven to Stanville so many times, she thought her car could automatically make it without her help. She checked the time and sped up. It wouldn't hurt to be a little early, because there was always a big crowd on Easter Sunday.

Sam was ready when she went to his house, looking very handsome in his best suit. He complimented her on her new outfit, and she told him how handsome he looked.

They drove straight to the church, and the parking lot was almost full, even though they were early. They found seats near the back and watched as the church filled to standing room only.

Sunlight filtered through stained-glass windows, filling the church with jewellike colors. Easter lilies lined the raised section behind which the choir, in rich wine-colored robes awaited the entrance of the minister.

In this magical setting, it was easy to believe Jesus had performed all the miracles put forth in the Bible. Certainly, for Chelsea, it took no stretch of the imagination.

As they stood for the doxology, Chelsea became aware of one person two rows ahead, who was taller than anyone in his row. His broad shoulders and black hair were familiar, and when he turned his face so that his profile showed, she knew it was Greg. Was he a member, or just an Easter-only church-goer, as so many were today? Was he alone? Would he see her when he left?

Once they were seated, her attention was brought back to reality when Sam reached over and took her hand in his. He held it throughout the sermon. The minister spoke in a reso-nant voice, telling the story of the Resurrection to a hushed and reverent congregation.

Afterwards, the triumphant music soared, and they filed out into the vestibule, stopping only long enough to exchange a pleasant greeting with Dolores. She looked quite attractive in her Easter outfit, a decided improvement on the nondescript business suits she wore in Sam's office.

Chelsea caught sight of Greg out of the corner of her eye; however, he didn't look at them as he left, apparently alone, and a glance at Sam told her he hadn't noticed Greg's pres-ence, either.

Outside, Sam did speak to some other people he knew and introduced Chelsea to them. Afterwards, they drove on to the Van Oghden mansion. "I like your minister very much," Chelsea said.

"Yes, he's quite good. Did you enjoy the service?"

"Of course. Did you?"

"Sure. Now I'm ready for some of that good barbecue."

There was a large crowd on the grounds of the mansion.

Children of all ages hunted Easter eggs hidden on the front lawn. In the back a huge tent had been set up, and the guests lined up for barbecue, beans, and coleslaw. Long tables were set up in the center, and they sat, happily enjoying their food.

Chelsea took a big bite of barbecued beef on a bun and washed it down with iced tea. "I was afraid all this would stop when Mr. Van Oghden died. Last fall wasn't it?"

"Yes, the middle of November. I understand he left a provision in his will that this was to continue. He has it financially underwritten."

"How nice. He was really the first citizen of New Mill, wasn't he?"

"Yes. Have you ever been in the mansion?"

"Last fall several of us came over when it was open for a tour to benefit the children's hospital. It's quite lovely, but I can't imagine what it would be like to actually live in such a large place."

"He had it professionally decorated, since he claimed his own taste was deplorable."

She chuckled. "It's a good thing he was willing to admit it. Some people would have gone on and made a mess of it."

They took their time, eating their fill, then visiting with people they knew, mostly Sam's acquaintances.

It was late afternoon when Chelsea decided she had better get back home. "I have preparations to make for school tomorrow," she explained. "The children have had a holiday, and they will be wild if we don't keep them busy."

She drove him back to his house, and he leaned over and kissed her before he scooted out of the car. Before he closed the door he told her good-bye. "I want your final decision on the wedding date no later than Friday night." With that, he closed the car door and turned to walk toward his house.

Chelsea drew in her breath, shocked, then she called out to him. "Is that an ultimatum?"

Sam's answer left no doubt. "I'm afraid so."

seven

Chelsea prayed quite a bit about Sam's ultimatum, but the week's work loomed ahead, and she had to put the problem aside for the present.

The sun beamed down in all its glory Monday morning. As she drove to school, Chelsea had a real attack of spring fever. What she longed to do was sit in the park and soak up the sun.

She pulled into the school parking lot and entered the building to the familiar smell of chalk dust, gym sweat, and a mixture of orange peel and peanut butter from the cafeteria. Sometimes, when she left the building at the end of the day, she wondered if she smelled that way, too.

This was her week to be recess monitor, and she congratulated herself on her good luck weather-wise. The children had spring fever, too, and she tried not to push them too hard, since she knew exactly how they felt.

She had brought her library book along, and she finished it while she ate lunch. After school, she took it by the library. Ginnie's after-school assistant was sitting at the desk, checking out books, and Ginnie was standing on a ladder, replacing books on the shelves.

As soon as she saw Chelsea, she climbed down and greeted her. "I need a break. Let's go out to the back stoop and sit in the sun. How about a Coke?"

"Fine." Chelsea followed her to the back where she got a couple of bottles out of the Coke machine.

Ginnie sat on a step and indicated a place beside her. "I never think about how musty the library smells until we have a day like today, then I can hardly stand to stay inside." She took a swig of Coke. "How was school today?"

"Not bad. The kids have spring fever, and so do I."

"Yeah, me too. How was your date Friday night?"

"Fine, I had a great time."

"And how is Sam?"

"Oh, he's fine. Busy as ever."

"Where did you eat?"

"You mean Friday night?"

"Yes." Ginnie sipped her Coke and leaned back on the stair railing.

"We ate at Barcarolle."

"You did? I thought Sam didn't like that kind of food."

"He doesn't. I was with Greg."

"What?" Ginnie sat up straight.

Chelsea told her what had happened. "I did go out with Sam on Saturday night. We ate at Bramwell's Inn. In fact, we saw your parents there."

"Did you tell Sam about your date with Greg?"

"No, of course not." Now she was beginning to feel guilty again.

"Don't you think you should have? I mean, you are engaged to Sam."

"I know, but Greg is just a friend. Besides, I was put out with Sam for canceling our date at the last minute."

"Yeah, I know how you feel, but just the same, Chelsea, it doesn't seem quite right."

"Well," Chelsea reasoned, "I wouldn't feel as if I had to tell Sam if I had dinner with you, and Greg is just a friend, like you."

Ginnie stared at her. "Chelsea Morgan, Greg isn't anything like me, and you know it. Furthermore, you know good and well you can't be just friends with a big, gorgeous hunk like that." She shook her head sadly. "Face it, honey, you're going to have to make a choice."

That wasn't what Chelsea wanted to hear. She regarded her friend solemnly. Neither of them spoke while she finished her Coke. Then she rose to go. "I can't," she said in a choked voice. "I can't make a choice."

"You'd better go home and think about it," Ginnie advised, holding the door for her. "There's no way you can have both of them at the same time, and I think you know it."

The wind had switched to the north, and the cold breeze had changed the weather. Chelsea walked out to her car, feeling numb all over. As she drove, she noticed little bits of trash swirling up. Clouds covered the sun, giving the landscape a bleak look.

Her mood changed with the weather. Was Ginnie right? Just because you were engaged, you didn't have to give up all your friends, did you?

Home at last, she took in her briefcase filled with school papers, and put them on her desk. Fortunately, there wouldn't be too many papers to grade tonight.

She opened her mail, containing a letter from her mother with a clipping about one of her friends who had announced her engagement. Her mother had added a note of her own. "He can't compare with Sam," she wrote.

Chelsea tossed the letter aside and paced the floor. What would Sam's reaction be if she told him she had been out with Greg? She rolled her eyes toward the ceiling. There was no doubt he would be upset.

She decided not to think about it anymore today. She would

do what she always advised her students to do, go right in and get her homework done before supper.

After dinner, she set out her clothes for the next day. Something warm and suitable for playground duty.

Everything considered, she was in a pretty good mood when she arrived at school the next morning.

She went back to the teachers' lounge where several of her friends were having doughnuts and coffee. They were talking about the school bully, Don Budge. Each of them had her own story.

Don was big for his age and slow. Maybe being a bully was the only way he could make himself feel superior, but that was no excuse. Ellen was especially angry. "When that cute new kid from Kansas City came in on his first day at school, he sat down right next to Don." She made a wry face. "I knew there would be trouble, and it started even before recess."

"I know what you mean," Phyllis said. "He's going to injure someone if we aren't careful."

Chelsea joined in the conversation. "I'm playground monitor this week, and I'll keep an eye on him, so don't worry." She finished her coffee just as the bell rang.

Later, she would make a note of the date. April the eighteenth, one of the worst days of her life.

When the bell for recess rang, she put on her heavy jacket, and went out to the playground. Actually, it wasn't so terribly chilly. The wind had stopped, and there was even a watery sun beginning to peek out.

She looked around for Don Budge and positioned herself near him, just in case there should be any trouble. The new boy, a cute little redhead named Jimmy Branskovitch, was playing nearby, minding his own business.

The recess period was half over, and so far uneventful,

when without warning, Don Budge gave Jimmy a shove and said, "We don't want any dumb redheads from Kansas City around here!"

At first, Chelsea didn't notice. She was engrossed in watching one of the little second-grade blonds chasing a cute second-grade boy.

They start early, she thought.

Jimmy Branskovitch turned out to be tougher than any of them suspected. He called Don a name and pushed him back. The fight was already on by the time Chelsea became aware of it. The two boys circled for position, like roosters at a cockfight, and almost immediately, the other students gathered around to goad them on.

Don gave a quick jab, catching Jimmy on the shoulder. Jimmy punched back, and Don managed to dodge. Another punch from Don caught Jimmy on the cheek, and it started swelling immediately. Jimmy kicked, and landed one on Don's shin.

Infuriated, Don went after him like a pit bull.

All the time, Chelsea was yelling, "Stop this instant! Do you hear me? Break it up!"

Of course, they paid no attention, and the other kids kept egging them on. Jimmy was hurt, and Chelsea panicked.

She turned to the nearest little girl and screamed, "Janice! Quick, run in and get Mr. Culpepper!" She was horrified as blood spurted from Jimmy's nose.

"Stop it, Don!" she yelled, but there was no stopping him now.

Mr. Culpepper hurried out the door, looking like a black thundercloud ready to erupt. He half ran down the steps, and waded right into the crowd of screaming children.

They parted as soon as they saw their principal, and their

shouts died down. Mr. Culpepper took hold of Don Budge's ear and propelled him, twisting and turning in pain, back toward the building.

They were halfway up the stairs when it happened. The principal grabbed at his chest and collapsed, and as they all watched in horror, he very slowly rolled back down the steps to the ground.

Chelsea was the first to reach him. "Oh no! No! Please don't. . ." Her voice was no more than a low moan. He was an awful gray color. She looked up in desperation to find two teachers approaching. "Call an ambulance, quick!" she shouted.

The gym teacher knelt beside Mr. Culpepper and started CPR. At the same time, Chelsea herded the children into the building. Mercifully, the bell rang just then, making her job easier.

It seemed like forever, but actually it had been only five minutes, when she heard the high-pitched sound of the ambulance siren. The attendants were a marvel of efficiency, as they went about their business. They quickly dispatched their equipment and went to work as their patient lay there on the ground. Not a second was wasted.

Little faces pressed against the school windows, watching the drama below. The attendants loaded Mr. Culpepper onto a stretcher and whisked him away in the ambulance.

It was lunchtime when they heard the sad news. Mr. Culpepper was already dead when the ambulance had arrived at the hospital.

Later, Chelsea would wonder how she ever managed to make it through the rest of the day. Certainly, it took an act of will to keep her mind on the schoolwork. She musn't think of Mr. Culpepper or the events leading up to his death.

When the final bell rang, the children erupted from the building with their usual noisy explosion of energy. As for Chelsea, she was trembling so, she had to sit down for a few minutes to collect herself.

Finally, she took a deep breath and walked blindly out the front door. Her head was down as she tried to conceal the depth of her emotion from any children who were still around. She wavered as she reached the stairs where poor Mr. Culpepper had collapsed.

She made her way down the steps slowly, blinking back the tears that started with a burning feeling behind her eyeballs. She managed to drive home with the utmost effort, somehow holding it all back numbly until she rounded the corner leading to her apartment building, and there she saw a sight that made her feelings come back to life.

Greg's big semi was parked right in front of her entrance, and he was leaning casually against it. His expression brightened when he caught sight of her car, and he walked over to her parking spot and opened her door for her.

Emotions warred crazily inside her. She wanted to laugh with joy at seeing Greg, and she wanted to run inside where she could be alone and sob her heart out. That would have to wait, though.

Greg saw inside her head immediately. He peered at her anxiously. "Something's wrong, isn't it?" They hurried along the walkway to the entrance, and he held the door for her.

She didn't answer his question. "I didn't expect to see you," she said, fitting her key into the lock. Inside, she put their jackets on a chair, and they walked toward the sofa.

"What's happened, Chelsea? Are you all right?"

Now the tears started. She tried to hold back, but it was no use. His arms went around her, and she sobbed on his shoulder, trying to talk, but not doing too well. "M–M–Mr. Culpepper. He's d–dead."

"You mean the old gentleman I met? The principal?"

She dabbed at her eyes and sniffled, pulling away from Greg's shoulder.

Greg eyed her with a serious expression. "I had no idea you were so fond of him."

"Sure, I liked him. He was a good person, but he's dead, and it's my fault."

"How could that be?"

She told him about the fight, and about sending for Mr. Culpepper to stop it. Her voice cracked as she talked about it, and she wrung her hands nervously.

"I knew he had heart trouble. He almost died before my very eyes only a few weeks ago. A chicken bone lodged in a student's throat during lunch, and he turned blue before Mr. Culpepper performed a Heimlich maneuver and dislodged it. Poor Mr. Culpepper was so upset afterwards he had to lie down before he finally recovered.

"I should have been able to handle that fight myself some way."

Now Greg put his arms around her. "Calm down, honey. You did the right thing. Mr. Culpepper was just doing his job. Who knows, if you hadn't sent for him, that young kid might have been seriously injured, then think how you would feel."

She clung to him. "Oh, Greg, I'm glad you're here."

His arms tightened around her, and he gave her a big squeeze. "Now, brighten up, will you? I'm sorry about Mr. Culpepper, but believe me, there's no reason to blame yourself."

She took a deep breath and smiled at him. "You're a good friend, Greg. It seems as if you're always there when I need you."

He loosened his hold on her, and she looked up into his eyes. "Just why are you here? And would you like a cup of coffee?"

"Sure." He followed her into the kitchen and watched as she prepared the coffee. "One of my drivers who lives here called this morning and said his kid was in the hospital for an emergency appendectomy. He was due to make the run to Fort Worth overnight, and I told him I'd take over.

"I came over to see if I could do anything for him before I left. He's a basket case. Seems the kid has all sorts of problems. He's been delicate since birth. He's not a good surgical risk."

She filled a couple of mugs with coffee, and they carried them into the living room. "He's lucky to have such a caring boss. Not every employer would be so kind."

"Maybe not, but I wouldn't have much of a company without my drivers." He gave her a warm grin. "I couldn't very well come over here and not see you, could I?"

"I hope not. You were just what I needed." She took a sip of the hot coffee. "I think I'm beginning to revive now. So how long will you be gone?"

"Not long. Four or five days. I won't be gone any longer than I have to. Actually, I'll enjoy it. Texas is beautiful this time of year. It's really warm, and the bluebonnets are in bloom, fields of blue as far as the eye can see. In town, the tulips and azaleas will be in bloom around every house."

"Sounds nice. Too bad I can't go with you."

A flicker of light sparked in his eyes at the thought. "Too bad. You're welcome anytime, you know."

She laughed. "Do any of the men take their girlfriends along?"

"It wouldn't surprise me."

"And do you go along with it?"

"I'm mainly concerned with delivering the goods on time and obeying all the safety rules of the road."

"And how about you? Do you ever take a girlfriend along on a cross-country drive?"

He chuckled. "The girls I know aren't usually available for such things. You know, some of the guys take their wives. They can be very useful in helping to keep them awake during the long night hours. That's the big problem on the road."

"I should think it would be very dangerous, driving at night and falling asleep behind the wheel."

"It is. They're supposed to pull over and take a nap when they feel themselves getting sleepy."

"I'm sure it must get very lonely."

"Yeah, I suppose so, but most of us have friends all along the way." He finished his coffee. "That's one of the things that makes it enjoyable, seeing old friends every once in a while."

"I never thought of that. Do you mean old school friends, or what?"

"No, just local people you meet. You'd have to see them to know what I mean."

"I suppose so." She finished her coffee and set her cup down. "More coffee?"

He shook his head. "Not for me. I'd better be on my way." He stood and started toward the door. "I'm glad we had this chance to talk. You are okay now, aren't you?"

"Yes, thanks to you." She stood at the door with him, feeling so much more inside than she could possibly express. "You are a good friend, Greg, or did I say that?"

He had both her hands in his. "You said it, and I'm glad to hear it again."

"Take care of yourself on the road," she admonished lamely.

"Yes, I will. I'll call you when I get back," and as if it were an afterthought, he leaned down and cupped her face in his hands. He looked deep into her eyes, and then he kissed her.

It was a gentle kiss, not much more than an ordinary good-bye kiss, except that it lasted just a little bit too long to be the kiss of a mere friend.

Chelsea felt the warm rush of her blood as his lips met hers, and it took all of her reserves to keep from clinging to him. Her voice sounded quite unnatural to her as she said, "Good-bye."

She thought she detected a heightened timbre to his voice, too, when he said, "So long."

eight

Chelsea's week at school went along as before, except that the children seemed more subdued.

There was Mr. Culpepper's funeral to attend, and she went in a group with the other teachers. A drizzly day didn't help. Somehow she managed to squelch the feelings of guilt that rose up as she sat through the somber ceremony. *Greg is right, of course,* she reminded herself.

A replacement was found for a new principal from Buffalo, a young man inexperienced but with excellent credentials. He was to arrive the following week. In the meantime, they managed to get along as best they could.

Her weekend date with Sam went about as usual, except that Sam brought up the subject she dreaded again. "So what did you decide about the wedding date?"

"Oh, dear, how awful of me. I had such a hectic week I didn't even think about it until now. I promise I'll let you know next weekend."

Sam stared at her, plainly exasperated.

She explained about the tragedy at school and all the hectic problems that arose from it.

He offered his condolences over Mr. Culpepper's death, and he made every effort to please her. He even apologized again for last weekend's broken date. *All in all,* she mused, *Sam is a good person.*

Unfortunately, she found herself being more and more bored when they were together. Their conversation always followed the same track. She would tell him about her week at school.

Then, he would tell her about business. When they first met, she hadn't found this so tiresome.

The names of all his clients were well-known to her, even though she didn't know most of them personally. Maybe this was why he felt he could tell her about them without actually revealing any confidences.

It was during just such a conversation that she missed yet another opportunity to tell him about her friendship with Greg McCormick.

"It was because of my new client, Greg McCormick, that I had to cancel our date last Friday night. You met him in my office, if you'll remember."

"Uh, yes, I do." Her conscience was urging her on. "I meant to tell you. . ." She hesitated, trying to think how she could put it.

"Tell me what?"

"I. . .uh, I was upset at the time, but I got over it." She just couldn't come out with it. What a coward!

"I don't blame you, honey. It was such short notice, but it was important. You know I couldn't risk losing an important client by failing to deliver so soon. Yes sir, that one will pay off in the long run. He's a good businessman."

And so it went. It was the last good opportunity to tell him, and she missed it.

At the end of the evening, Sam reminded her again about the wedding date, and his voice sounded cold. "Next week for sure. Do you understand?"

&

Her mother called Sunday night, as she often did, just to keep in touch. After the preliminaries were over, she went straight to the important stuff, at least for her. "How's Sam?"

"Oh, fine. About the same."

"I wanted to tell you about Marcia's wedding."

"Yes, you sent me a clipping."

"Well, it was just lovely. Four bridesmaids and four groom's attendants, a flower girl, and two young boys to light the candles. Her dress must have cost a fortune. A long train, the works. Of course, the groom wasn't much to look at, kind of a homely fellow. Not nearly as good-looking as Sam."

"I'm sure it was lovely," Chelsea said agreeably.

Her mother wasn't through, though. There was still the reception to report on. "I never saw so much food in my life. Two long tables. All kinds of fancy cheese. Fruit heaped up in the center. Little sandwiches. Even shrimp. That stuff costs an arm and a leg, you know. They'll be paying for that a long time." She caught her breath then went on.

"You should have seen the wedding cake. Three tiers! All white, of course, and there was a devil's food groom's cake, too. Delicious. Oh, and a silver punch bowl, with refreshing pink punch. My, it was something!"

Now, her mother's voice took on another tone. "Well, Chelsea, it's almost May. Have you set your wedding date yet?"

"No, I really haven't given it much thought. I've had other things on my mind. Mr. Culpepper's death was so traumatic. There was a lot of turmoil at school. We do have a new principal coming in next week, though. I'll get busy and see if I can make a decision. There's no rush."

"I don't know how you can say that. It's only a little over a month until June. You should have all your plans made by now. You and Sam haven't had trouble, have you?"

"No, Mother, but I'm just not that anxious to get married. There's plenty of time."

She heard her mother sigh.

"Thanks for calling, Mother."

Her mother reluctantly ended the conversation, and Chelsea lay back on the bed, exhausted. Her mother was right, of course. Time was speeding by. She must set the date and complete her plans or else end the engagement.

Had Sam guessed how reluctant she was to go ahead with the wedding? He was pressing her hard about the date, and she could hardly blame him.

She couldn't even talk to Ginnie about it anymore. Ginnie had lost patience with her. She felt, as her mother did, that Chelsea should marry Sam right away.

Ginnie had stopped by on her way home from her mother's. "I declare, Chelsea, I don't know what's the matter with you. Sam's going to find someone else if you're not careful."

"I can't help it. I'd rather not get married at all than marry someone I'm not sure of."

Ginnie frowned. "You'll live to regret it."

"Maybe not. I can always support myself, and there are worse things than not getting married."

"Yes, like marrying someone terrible, but there's nothing wrong with Sam. Or, at least, I don't think there is. Is there something you're not telling me?"

"No. Sam's okay. You'll have to admit he's kind of boring, though."

"Well, what do you expect? Do you think some dashing movie star is going to swoop down to Stanville and carry you away with him?"

Chelsea laughed softly at the thought. "Maybe I'm waiting for some dashing truck driver to swoop down and carry me off."

Ginnie's expression became serious. "So that's it!" She shook her head sadly. "Oh, Chelsea, what a mistake. You hardly know that man."

"You're right, but I can't get him out of my mind."

"Oh, I could just shake you. Has he ever been married?"

"No, he hasn't. I asked him."

"Well, there you are. He's probably in his mid-thirties. He's not the marrying kind. I'll bet he's known plenty of women. After you, he'll go on to his next conquest."

Ginnie's conversation had made her feel worse than ever. Once she was gone, Chelsea paced the floor a long time. What was it Greg had said? "I'm one of those nimble bachelors who somehow manages to avoid the big capitulation." Ginnie's words sounded more sensible all the time.

❧

The following week found the school swept up in the excitement of a new principal. Thomas Garner arrived on Wednesday, looking more like one of the local college students than the principal of the grade school.

First, there was an assembly to welcome him. He was a sandy-haired man of about thirty, at most. Although he was clean shaven, Chelsea suspected he would look dashing with a beard.

His clothes were casual, navy slacks and a well-worn blue tweed jacket. Perhaps that wouldn't have seemed casual, she reminded herself, if she hadn't been used to seeing Mr. Culpepper in a dark suit.

The assembly was fairly brief, and he said a few words that established just the right tone, not too serious, but not flippant either. After that, he met separately with each member of the faculty, a shrewd gesture to get him off to a good start. After Mr. Culpepper, whose age and experience gave him a certain dignity, Mr. Garner was not what Chelsea had expected.

She must not have hidden her amazement very well, because he chuckled. "You weren't expecting a mere upstart to take over Mr. Culpepper's job, were you?"

"I understand you're very well-qualified, and that counts for a lot," Chelsea replied.

"Despite his age, Mr. Culpepper appears to have been an excellent administrator."

"Yes, and he was a good man. He had the best interests of the students at heart, and he always worked hard for them, even though his health was not good at the end. We'll miss him," she said simply.

"I hope you won't be expecting another Mr. Culpepper. I'll have to be my own man. This is the perfect time to make any changes that would improve the school."

He sat forward and regarded her earnestly. "Sometime in the next week or ten days, I would like to have any suggestions you might have. Will you give it some thought?"

"Yes, I'll be glad to."

A satisfied smile crossed Chelsea's face as she made her way to her classroom. She liked Thomas Garner already. And for the first time since that awful day when Mr. Culpepper died, she had a feeling of well-being.

She stopped in the library after school to pick up a book, and told Ginnie about him. "He's quite young for a school principal, but he seems to have a lot of sense, and he's supposed to be well-qualified. I liked him right away."

Ginnie cut through to the heart of the matter. "Is he married?"

Chelsea laughed at her. "Really, Ginnie! I don't know, but I'll find out."

"It's the least you can do," Ginnie said cheerfully. "I haven't given up yet."

≈

That night, Chelsea had a call from Greg. "Hi. I'm back from Texas, and I'm a-lookin' to take a pretty little filly out for some grub. Just friends, of course."

Chelsea laughed out loud. "Greg, that is the worst Western accent I've ever heard."

"We don't appreciate sassy women down in the Lone Star

State," he said with mock sternness.

"Sorry about that," she said contritely. "You did say just friends, didn't you? What night?"

"How about Friday?"

"That should be fine. Casual, I presume."

"Just about as casual as you can get."

"Okay," she agreed.

"About 5:45?"

"That sounds good." She replaced the receiver. *It was just the sort of evening a couple of old friends could enjoy without causing talk,* she mused.

She made a note in her date book. "Friday at 5:45," she wrote. And then a troubling thought crossed her mind. She and Sam usually went out on Friday nights.

Now, what should she do? Sam frequently called at the last minute, knowing she was always available, as well she should be. She sighed. This could present a real problem. However, she would just tell him she was too tired to go out because of all the new problems at school, and could they make it Saturday night?

On Thursday, Chelsea was able to find out that there was no Mrs. Garner. *That will be good news for Ginnie,* she thought. Now, she would have to think of some way to get them together.

That night, she was going through her closet to see what she had that would do for her date with Greg the following night, when the telephone rang.

Ginnie's voice held a note of excitement. "He was in here today, Chelsea, and he's darling!"

"Who's darling?"

"Thomas Garner, of course. He checked out a whole bunch of books. He was really friendly, and he didn't even know me."

"Is that right? I was wondering how I could get you two together. I found out today there isn't any Mrs. Garner, so do your best."

"There isn't? All right! I know what he likes to read now, and I'll steer him onto some more books I think he'd like."

Ginnie changed the subject. "So, what are you doing this weekend? I guess you'll be going out with Sam tomorrow night, huh?"

"As a matter of fact, I have a date with Greg tomorrow night." She heard Ginnie gasp. "Now, don't get excited. It's just a real casual get-together between a couple of friends, that's all."

"But you usually go out with Sam on Friday nights."

"I know. I'll just have to tell him I'm too tired. There's no reason we can't go out on Saturday instead."

"But what if he finds out about Greg?"

"I don't think that's likely to happen. We'll be here in Stanville, and if I know Sam, he'll be working, so relax."

"Well, I give up. I can't talk any sense into you," Ginnie said with an air of resignation.

All the next day, Chelsea went through the motions of teaching, while at the same time, part of her was thinking of her date with Greg. Where would he take her? What would they do? Probably something she hadn't even thought of. He was nothing if not unpredictable.

Thomas Garner was the talk of the teacher's lounge. He seemed to have everyone's approval. Chelsea detected a note of proprietary interest from Phyllis. "I've never met a man I could be so comfortable with. We really got along well."

Yes, Chelsea thought, *I'll have to warn Ginnie not to waste any time.* Obviously, Phyllis had her eye on him, and she was right here under his nose all the time, too.

After school, she went home and straightened her apartment. Greg had said to be as casual as possible, so she got out her jeans and a T-shirt. At least, she knew they wouldn't be going to Barcarolle, but where could he be taking her?

He was right on time, and she went to answer the bell. He, too, was dressed casually, in jeans and a plaid shirt. "Howdy, partner," he said.

"Don't tell me," she said. "We're still doing the Texas bit." She ushered him into the living room. "Could I get you something before we leave?"

"No, thanks." He sat there looking ruggedly handsome, while she tried to figure out what he had in mind.

"Dare I ask where we're going?"

There was a mischievous twinkle in his eyes as he answered. "I couldn't very well take a pretty little filly like you to a saloon," he said. "We're going to a chili supper at my church in New Mill. That's why I made this such an early date."

He seemed to be in an exuberant mood for some reason, and she walked out to the car with him with mixed feelings. It was reassuring to know that he was taking her to a church function, but she hadn't expected it to be in New Mill. Actually, she reasoned, there was very little likelihood they would encounter Sam. He had never taken her to church, except on Easter, and he would undoubtedly be working.

As Greg pulled his car out onto the highway, he gave her a reassuring smile. "Relax. You're going to have fun."

"I'm sure I will. I didn't realize you were so active in your church."

"Of course. Tonight's chili supper is a fund-raiser to buy a new piano for the children's department."

Sam was an indifferent Christian. It was one thing that troubled Chelsea about him. Oh, he claimed to be willing to go to church with her whenever she wished, but faith didn't seem to have the same priority in his life as it did in hers.

"I haven't been to your church except for the Easter service, but I liked your minister very much."

Greg smiled. "He's the greatest. Does Sam belong to that church?"

"Yes, but I don't think he attends regularly. He's pretty busy, you know."

"Too busy for church?"

"I'm planning to change that when we're married."

"Good luck."

She didn't like the way this conversation was going. Talking about Sam to Greg was distinctly uncomfortable.

"Tell me about your trip to Texas."

"The best thing about it was that I saw a lot of old friends. I know people all along the way, and there's something about Texas folks. They're so warm and comfortable to be around. Nobody puts on airs, you know."

"Yes. Actually, you're kind of like a Texan yourself."

"Thanks. Well, the weather there is way ahead of ours. It was warm, the fields were full of bluebonnets. It's the prettiest time of year down there."

The barren scenery between Stanville and New Mill was a blur outside her window as she watched Greg's strong profile. She felt an inner completeness when she was with him, not unlike the security of owning a home with no mortgage.

Greg turned to her. "How was your day?"

"Can't complain. There were no fights, nobody got sick, and nobody wet their pants and had to go home."

Greg's eyebrows shot up. "That happens?"

"More often than you'd think."

She told him about the new principal. "I feel very good about him. He may be just what that school needs."

As they approached New Mill, Chelsea felt another twinge of guilt. Why was it she just couldn't turn down a date with

Greg? Was his friendship that important to her?

She glanced at his profile again. He was unbearably handsome. The guilt gave way to a little ache way down inside her. She took a deep breath. *Help me to be strong, Lord.*

There were already quite a few cars in the church parking lot. As they approached the entrance, the sounds of laughter and conversation wafted out to them.

Inside, they were greeted by several people who were in charge. Greg filled out a couple of name tags for them, made introductions, and they headed for the table where the chili was being dispensed.

Along the way, Greg was stopped by friends, anxious to meet Chelsea. It appeared he knew everyone in the room, and they were glad to see him. To Chelsea, it was almost like a family gathering.

There were tables set up around the room, and they joined several couples to eat their chili. It was Greg who said the brief, traditional blessing before they ate.

"Why is it, food that's made in large quantities is always so much better?" Chelsea asked.

Pat, a pretty blond sitting next to her, nodded her head in agreement. "I'll bet if I made chili for my family at home using their recipe, it wouldn't taste half as good."

Greg added hot sauce generously, and Chelsea nudged Pat. "You can tell he's just back from Texas."

"It would blow the top of my head off to eat that much hot sauce," Pat said.

"I reckon you Yankees aren't used to eatin' like real Texas hombres," Greg said, but he took a quick swig of his iced tea.

Pat's husband, Martin, rolled his eyes upward. "How long does it take him to get back to normal after one of these trips?"

Chelsea grinned. "Not long, I hope."

After they finished eating, they stopped to chat with other friends of Greg's. People arrived and left all during the evening, and by this time the room had reached capacity.

Chelsea's glance darted around the room. Surely Sam wouldn't come to this. She was surprised at how popular this simple entertainment was.

Greg noticed. "Are you looking for someone?"

"No. I was just amazed at what a crowd is here tonight."

"Yeah. It seems like all our events are fun. I think it's the people more than anything else. They just feel comfortable here. I'm surprised I never see Sam at any of these little get-togethers."

Did he sense her concern about Sam? "He keeps pretty busy most of the time."

"You mean he was too busy to take you out tonight?"

Chelsea swallowed hard. What was he getting at? "Oh, he called, but I told him I'd rather go out tomorrow night."

"I think we need to talk about this, Chelsea. I don't feel right about what we're doing."

Chelsea felt defensive now. "Is it so wrong for two friends to go out for a casual evening at a church function?"

"I'm not so sure we're just friends." He looked deep into her eyes with a serious expression.

Before she could speak, he continued. "I'm a Christian, and I take the marriage vows very seriously. An engagement is a trust between two people, which shouldn't be broken lightly."

"You're right, Greg. Perhaps I've been fooling myself. I have had feelings of guilt, but I somehow managed to convince myself there was nothing wrong with two good friends being together. Is that so bad?"

Greg's answer shook her deeply. "I thought we were more than friends. Oh, I know I've been more guilty than you but that was only because I was so sure Sam was wrong for you, and I had to help you see it." With that, he took her arm and moved toward the exit. "Let's get out of here."

As they neared the exit, Chelsea found herself face-to-face with a familiar person. With a sickening realization, she saw that Sam's secretary, Dolores Preston, had already recognized her.

nine

After a sleepless night, Chelsea started her Saturday morning as usual, cleaning her apartment, only this time she attacked her job as though she were killing snakes.

She had tossed and turned all night, trying to decide how best to handle the blowup that was sure to occur as soon as Dolores told Sam that she had seen Chelsea and Greg out on a date together.

The shock on Dolores's face when she met them leaving the church party was something Chelsea would remember a long time. Dolores had gasped and seemed puzzled at first, then angry. "Chelsea, I thought you were going out with Sam tonight." Then, when she saw Greg's hand under Chelsea's arm, she realized the two of them were together. "You know each other?"

The puzzled expression, and the shock, quickly turned to anger. "How could you?" With that she swept past them, before either of them could offer a word of explanation.

Chelsea had vacuumed the entire apartment and was in the midst of mopping the kitchen floor when she heard the doorbell. Who could that be at ten o'clock in the morning?

She hurried in to answer it.

Her heart sank at the sight of Sam looking very serious. "Oh, hello, Sam. Come on in."

He followed her into the living room. "We need to talk, Chelsea." His voice was steady and quiet. "I think you know why I'm here."

"I, uh. . .you mean about last night?"

He nodded silently.

"Yes, I thought so." She shifted her position uncomfortably. "You see, it was just a matter of two old friends spending an evening together. It had nothing to do with us."

"You and Greg McCormick are old friends?"

"Yes. I wanted to tell you, but I just couldn't come up with the right words."

"Apparently," he said dryly. "I thought I had introduced you two in my office."

"It was Greg who picked me up that afternoon when my car broke down."

"So that's it!" His eyes narrowed as though he were trying to guess what went on that day.

"It all seemed to be a series of coincidences. I wish I could tell you how it happened that we became friends, but I'm not sure myself. Each time I saw him, I thought I'd never see him again, and Sam, you have to believe me, I never actually made an attempt to see him on my own."

He was silent for a long time, and the silence hung between them like a cement wall.

Finally, he spoke. "I think I've known for a long time the wedding wasn't going to take place. Oh, I kept hoping, but I didn't know what had come between us. Now I know."

He started to rise, then he sat back down. "I think I may as well tell you what you're giving up besides me. I kept pushing you to marry me before the fourteenth for a good reason. You would have misunderstood my reason for wanting to marry you, if you had known everything."

"You did push me, and I hope you had a good reason."

"Herbert Van Oghden was my uncle. His will stipulated that I was to inherit the Van Oghden mansion if I were married within six months of his death. He died on November fourteenth, so that's why I was so adamant that we marry before May fourteenth."

Chelsea was speechless. Finally, she found her voice. "I don't know what to say, Sam. I'm sorry. It seems I've knocked you out of your inheritance."

"Yes. Some people might suggest we get married anyway, and then you could divorce me later, but I think I know you well enough to know you wouldn't be party to anything like that."

"No, I wouldn't. Why would he make such a stipulation?"

"He wanted his home to be passed down to the next generation. Actually, he never liked me. That's why I always worked so hard. I wanted to make a fortune on my own. He left everything else to the city, but since I was his only living relative, he did leave his home to me. I guess the city will get it now."

"Oh, Sam. I'm so sorry."

He left without another word, and Chelsea sat there in the morning shadows of her living room. Somehow, the gloom fit her mood. She thought of Sam, not so much with regret as with a feeling of emptiness. A big part of her life had changed.

There was guilt mixed in with her other emotions, too. She realized she hadn't been aboveboard with Sam for a long time. Strangely enough, it wasn't only Sam who had been deceived. She had actually deceived herself.

Finally, she slowly pulled herself out of her stupor and returned to her work in the kitchen. She wanted a shoulder to cry on, but there was no one she could call. Certainly not Ginnie. She would have to wait and talk to her when she was in a better mood.

She finished mopping the kitchen floor, then she did the laundry. As she did her chores, the gloom gradually lifted. *It's as if there's no life after Sam,* she told herself. There was still

Greg, and now she could get on with her life with a clear conscience.

Although she and her mother seldom called each other during the day, she decided this was a good time to give her the news, so she sat down and made the call.

Her mother seemed startled. "Oh, it's you, Chelsea." Her voice sounded nervous. "Is anything wrong?"

"I guess it's all in how you look at it," Chelsea answered vaguely. "Sam and I have broken up."

There was a shocked silence. When her mother's voice finally came on the line, Chelsea felt another pang of guilt. Her mother sounded distraught. "Oh, I've prayed you wouldn't make that mistake, honey. I can't imagine what came over you."

"Mother, I wish you wouldn't take on so. Sam isn't the only man in the world."

"Now what will you do?"

"I'll feel free to spend more time with Greg McCormick. He is a wonderful person, and I'm sure you would like him just as well as Sam if you knew him."

"Is he that truck driver?"

"He owns a large trucking company," Chelsea said quietly.

"I see. Well, whatever makes you happy, dear. That's all I ask."

"Couldn't you just come up for a short visit, so you could meet him?"

"Oh, I couldn't leave your Aunt Joanne."

Chelsea hesitated. Her mother did faithfully look after her only sister, Joanne, who had cancer. "Not even for a weekend?"

"Well, maybe that long, but no longer. We'll have to see how she is."

"Good," Chelsea said. "That settles it. I'll work out the details with you later."

"All right, dear. We'll settle on a date then."

As the day wore on, another thought occurred to Chelsea. How would all this affect Greg and Sam's business dealings? She didn't have long to wait to find out.

A phone call from Greg came about midafternoon. She had been in the middle of her new book, exhausted from her orgy of housecleaning. "Oh, Greg, how are you?"

"Fine. The question is, how are you? Any repercussions from last night's encounter with Sam's secretary?"

She told him about Sam's visit. "Of course, I feel bad about it, although I realize it's for the best. I should have told him some time ago that I didn't want to go through with the wedding, but I wasn't being very honest with myself."

"I know. I think I knew from the first day I met you that you and Sam were wrong for each other. It just took a while for you to realize it."

"Yes. I felt bad about the way it ended, but I don't suppose it would have been very pleasant no matter how it happened. You don't know the worst part. He was going to inherit the Herbert Van Oghden mansion if he married by May fourteenth. I can tell you he was devastated to lose out on that."

"I had no idea."

"Yes, Mr. Van Oghden was Sam's uncle, although they were never close."

"You might be interested to know Sam and I had lunch together."

Her eyes widened in surprise. "You did?"

"I called and invited him. We talked frankly. I let him know there hadn't been any kind of big affair going on behind his back, and I think he appreciated it."

"Yes, I'm glad he knows that. After all, we didn't deliberately set out to deceive him."

"I feel bad about it, too. I did deceive him by giving him

work to tie him up so I could be with you. I was desperately trying to rescue you from a marriage that would have been disastrous."

"I know. I just feel so bad about causing him to lose his inheritance. He really wanted that wonderful house."

"I'm sure he did. Is there any way we could help?"

"I don't think so. It's a little late for him to find another bride. Just a matter of weeks."

Greg was silent for some time. Finally, Chelsea spoke up. "Are you there, Greg?"

"I'm just thinking. Did you ever notice the way that secretary of his looks at him? I think she has a big crush on him."

"Well, she has always been very protective of him, even where I was concerned. If he was busy, Dolores would make excuses for him. Actually, I don't think she liked me, and I must admit I rather resented her."

"That tells you something right there. How about Sam? How did he feel about her?"

"Well, obviously he wasn't in love with her, or he wouldn't have asked me to marry him. I do know he was very dependent on her. He once said he couldn't manage without her."

"Maybe I'm wrong, but I think it's worth a try. What do you think? I'll work on Sam and you work on Dolores. There is still time for an elopement."

By the time they finished their conversation, Chelsea felt as if she owed Sam that much. She would give it a try. She called Dolores and invited her to brunch after church Sunday.

Dolores showed surprise at Chelsea's invitation. "You want to take me to brunch? You know I can't do anything to help you patch things up with Sam."

"Yes, I know. That part is final. I just want us to get to know each other better. How about it?"

"Well, all right. Where shall I meet you?"

"How about Marie's?"

"Okay, right after church."

Chelsea called Greg and told him what she had done.

He seemed pleased. "Good, it's worth a try, and now I need to know something."

"Yes, what is it?"

"I need to know how you feel about the symphony. Do you like that kind of music?"

"Well, of course. Unfortunately, I don't get to hear much of it, living in Stanville. Why do you ask?"

"Oh, I have an idea. I'll have to work out the details. I'll get back to you in a couple of days."

"Okay, but now you have my curiosity aroused."

"Well, be patient. I may spring something on you."

She smiled, thinking what an unpredictable soul he was. "I'll be holding my breath."

"Now, young lady. The crucial question. What kind of mood are you really in? I've been afraid all of this would have you feeling depressed."

"I'm okay. Really. I did feel bad earlier, but I'm getting better all the time. No need to worry."

"I don't need to come over there and cheer you up?"

"No, I'm not about to jump out a window or anything. Actually, I'm feeling more relieved than anything else. Now I can get on with my life without feeling guilty about my lack of feelings for Sam. Did he seem terribly upset?"

"Naturally, but he's taking it better than I would. I think he's known for some time your feelings had changed."

"Well, I guess things could have ended in a much worse way."

"Yes. Thanks for calling."

❧

Chelsea got an early start Sunday morning. She set out for

New Mill in a good mood. The weather was warm and breezy, and she took a deep breath of the fragrant clean air. She felt good about her mission. Somehow she knew she was doing the right thing.

Help me to pull this off, Lord, so that Dolores will know she has a chance with Sam.

She glanced around upon entering the church, hoping to see Greg somewhere. Actually, he came in right behind her, and sat down beside her. She smiled at him and mouthed a silent hello.

He reached over and surreptitiously squeezed her hand.

They quietly listened to the sermon. The minister quoted Romans 8:28: "We know that all things work together for good to them that love God, to them who are the called according to his purpose."

As Chelsea listened, she thought how all this applied to her and Greg. Their chance meeting somehow worked to prevent her from making a bad mistake. Now they had the opportunity to bring two people together who belonged with each other. *You just had to trust in God, and try to do the right thing,* she mused. *Somehow, it would all turn out for the best.*

She and Greg left together after the services were over. He walked with her to her car and opened the door for her. "I'll call you later this afternoon," he said. "Good luck."

"Thanks." She flashed him a big smile, and drove off toward the restaurant.

Marie's was a tearoom, very popular with the after-church crowd. It was pretty, with pink and green decor, using a Victorian motif. As she waited, Chelsea looked over a menu. Quiche, pasta, fancy salads, hot rolls, the usual tearoom foods, and irresistible desserts.

Dolores entered, looking more attractive than usual.

They were seated at a table near the window.

"I'm glad you could join me," Chelsea said.

Reading over the menu, Dolores seemed reserved. "This looks good. I think I'll have quiche."

The waitress took their orders and poured coffee.

Chelsea realized she wouldn't get any help with this, so she dove right in. "Sam came by yesterday, and we talked. He said he had known for some time the wedding wasn't going to take place."

"Really?" Dolores's green eyes widened.

"Yes. We were all wrong for each other. Sam needs someone who can share his love for his business. I always resented the time he spent on it."

For the first time, Chelsea realized Dolores was a very pretty girl, with the sun from the window shining on her red hair. All this time, Chelsea had hardly noticed how she looked, sitting in Sam's office. Perhaps Sam thought of her the same way, just part of the office equipment.

"I didn't realize how wrong I was for Sam until I met Greg. For a long time, I considered Greg just a friend. He was the one I needed to talk to when something went wrong, and he was the one I wanted to share my happiness with during the good times."

"You should have told Sam sooner."

"I know, and I blame myself constantly for that. You see, I didn't deliberately set out to deceive Sam, I actually deceived myself."

The waitress arrived with the food, and their conversation stopped momentarily as they sampled it. "The quiche is delicious," Dolores said.

"So is my omelet." Chelsea continued. "Sam needs someone now more than ever. Someone to take my place."

Dolores regarded her with raised eyebrows. "You're not suggesting I try to fix Sam up with a friend. I couldn't—"

"No," Chelsea broke in, "that isn't what I had in mind. I was hoping you. . .well, Sam is very dependent on you. He once told me he couldn't get along without you. I think he cares more for you than you realize."

"Me? Oh, I hardly think so."

"Come on, Dolores. Why wouldn't he? You're a very pretty young woman, and. . ."

Dolores, wide-eyed, nearly choked on her coffee.

Before she could say anything, Chelsea continued. "Sam is a very desirable bachelor. As soon as the word gets out that we have broken up, you can imagine how he is going to be pursued. There isn't much time to waste."

"Oh, Chelsea. Do you think I could?"

"As I see it, Dolores, you have to let him know how you feel. Go for it."

To Chelsea's astonishment, tears sprang up in Dolores's eyes. She turned away, and dabbed at them with a tissue.

Chelsea finished her coffee and picked up the check.

They walked out together, and Dolores thanked her warmly. "You're. . ." The right words just didn't come.

"Good luck." Chelsea turned and walked to her car.

ten

It was only a few weeks until school would be out for the year. Still, that meant so much had to be crowded into such a short time. The teachers would have to wind up the year's work, give tests, and evaluate the students.

From the first, Chelsea had been able to tell who would make it in her class and who would have to be held back another year. Not that there was any stigma to being held back. It merely meant the youngster was immature.

That first day, she had picked out Tiffany, the little blond who was always gazing up at the ceiling or looking out the window when she explained the assignment for the next day.

Barry had sucked his fingers the whole time he was in class. The poor kid was a nervous wreck. He couldn't cope with any kind of challenge.

Then there was Al. Poor Al, so hyperactive he couldn't sit still for a minute. Not long enough to read the directions on a test, nor could he concentrate long enough to do his reading lesson.

She hated to give them the bad news, and sometimes their parents argued with her, insisting their little darlings were smarter than any of the other children. Oh, well, it was part of the job, and it was for their own good.

❧

A soft spring breeze riffled her hair as Chelsea walked from the parking lot around to the front of the library. She felt a sudden freedom of spirit, as though a weight had been lifted from her shoulders.

School was out for the day, and she carried a book to return. She hadn't yet told Ginnie about her breakup with Sam.

Ginnie's assistant was manning the desk, and Ginnie was in the back, opening a box of new books.

She looked up as Chelsea entered. "Hi." She held up a couple of new books. "Aren't these beautiful? It just kills me to have to put them on the shelves and see them come back all dirty and scuffed."

"Yes, it does seem a shame."

"So, what's new with you today?"

"I have some news, but first you have to promise you won't mention this to a soul. This is strictly confidential."

Ginnie stared with sudden interest. "I promise."

"Okay, you're looking at a free woman. I'm no longer engaged."

Ginnie's countenance took on a shocked expression. "You and Sam have broken up? Tell me what happened."

Chelsea told her about encountering Sam's secretary at the chili supper, then she told her about his visit Saturday morning.

"I'm surprised he took it as well as he did."

"Yes, that's Sam. Civilized to the end."

"But why is that such a big secret?"

"It just is, and it's important. I'll tell you why later, maybe after school is out. Now, don't forget. You promised. Anyway, the important thing is that Sam is no longer in the picture. I'm free to go out with Greg whenever I wish."

"Well, what's done is done. Now it's time to get on with your life," Ginnie said briskly.

"You're right, and if I were you, I wouldn't spend too much time hiding out back here after school. You might miss you-know-who, and I hate to tell you, but Phyllis Simecca has her eye on him."

Ginnie made a face. "Oh, she would." She held out one of

the new books. "This looks like something you would like."

"Thanks." Chelsea glanced through it. "I think I will take it."

"Good. I'll go up to the desk with you. I have to enter it in the computer."

Ginnie sent her assistant out to sort the new books, and she manned the desk, entering the new book into the computer. She handed it to Chelsea. "Enjoy. I'll see you later."

"Thanks." Chelsea waved good-bye.

As she drove home, she thought about her chat with Ginnie. She had sensed a certain reserve about her friend's acceptance of the news. There had been no input from Ginnie's side. Just a brisk "get on with your life."

She thought of Greg. He had said they were more than friends. She mustn't forget that. Even so, all that was far from a proposal of marriage. In the meantime, she would have to live with Ginnie's and her mother's skepticism, and she would have to pray that they were wrong.

She made out her reports and was prepared for the parents' conferences on Wednesday. That was a revelation sometimes when she saw what kind of families some of her students came from. Sometimes it was sad, always interesting.

On Tuesday night, she had an unexpected visitor. She answered the doorbell, peeking through the viewhole first. Her heart gave a pleasant surge, then she quickly unlocked the door.

"Oh, hello, Greg. This is an unexpected pleasure." She ushered him into the living room.

"I hope this isn't a bad time," he said. "I was passing through, and I needed to talk to you about something." He sat down on the sofa. "How's your mood?"

"Oh, just fine," she assured him. "I've been so busy at school I haven't had time to brood over my broken engagement."

"That's good. I was hoping that was the case. Now," his

voice took on a different tone, "I have a proposition for you."

"What kind?" Chelsea held her breath. Now that her engagement was broken, and Greg had told her he considered them more than friends. . .

"You remember I asked if you would like to attend the symphony. Well, it's all arranged. Are you free this weekend?"

"Yes, but. . ."

"No buts. It's all set. We'll drive over to Bismarck right after lunch Saturday, and come back on Sunday."

She started to protest, but he cut her off. "Now, give me a chance to explain. We're spending the night with some old friends of mine. I promise you'll like them. You'll have your own room, and if I know Martha, we'll have the best meal you've ever tasted."

"That sounds like an offer I couldn't refuse. I had no idea you were making all these plans."

He chuckled, pleased at her reaction. "I felt like I should produce something more elegant than the church chili supper."

"I loved the chili supper, but this sounds absolutely exciting. What time should I be ready?"

"I'll pick you up about one. Is that okay?"

"Fine. I'll be looking forward to it."

He rose to go. "I'd better let you get back to what you were doing."

She followed him to the door, and he bent to kiss her goodbye. His light kiss made her catch her breath, and she circled his neck with her arms. His second kiss was warm and slow, lingering delightfully as he pressed her close.

She moved her arms away from his neck and stepped back, a little breathlessly. "Thanks for coming by," she murmured, holding the door for him. She didn't trust herself to linger in his arms any longer.

Chelsea was still breathless when she locked the door and

went back to her bedroom. What a guy. First a chili supper, then the symphony. There was so much more there than she had dreamed the first time she met him. Had she finally met the perfect man? He seemed almost too good to be true.

She finally roused herself and returned to reality, going over to the closet to pick out what she should wear tomorrow. Something extra nice, since it was parents' day.

She settled on her navy suit with the frilly white blouse and her high-heeled pumps. Her feet would kill her before the day was over, but it was for a good cause. She still had her comfortable shoes in a drawer, just in case she couldn't make it through the day.

As she was finishing her report cards, she had a call from Ginnie.

"You'll never guess who I saw at the grocery store," she said, and her voice sounded like a teenager's. "You were right when you told me it was a great place to meet men. There he was, looking like an intellectual football player, wandering up and down the aisle as if he were lost."

"An intellectual football player?" Chelsea tried to picture it, but all she saw in her mind's eye was Thomas Garner pushing a basket.

Ginnie went on. "He recognized me immediately and asked if I knew where the Mexican foods were. I took him right over, and we had a nice chat. Do you have any good Mexican recipes?"

"Not really, but I could look some up."

"You might bear that in mind. It wouldn't hurt to try some, just in case I ever get to the point where I want to have him over for dinner. Do you have any plans for next weekend?"

"As a matter of fact, I do. I'll tell you about it later."

"I was just thinking maybe I should have a party and invite you and Greg and Thomas, if you were free."

"That sounds like a good idea, but why don't you wait until the following weekend, and I'll have the party. It would look better that way, since I know him from school."

"All right. You may have a good idea there, and I'll bring whatever you want."

"Okay, you can bring your pecan pie. If that doesn't do the trick, he's hopeless."

"You have a deal." Her voice held a lilt. "That poor fellow doesn't have a chance."

"You're right. I'm glad you called."

Ginnie said good night, and Chelsea went back to work, getting ready for tomorrow's parents' conferences. She never knew what to expect, and sometimes it was a good thing. She'd made up her mind a long time ago that children were easier to handle than their parents.

Finally she finished the last report card and went to bed, satisfied that she was well-prepared for the next day.

The individual conferences went about as she had expected. There were parents whose children had received bad report cards and who refused to believe their little darlings were getting a fair chance. One mother became quite belligerent and threatened to pull her son out of school.

After Chelsea talked to her calmly, pointing out various things which indicated the boy was simply immature and not stupid, his mother managed to become a bit more reasonable.

If only there were more parents like little Suzanne's, who took an active interest in everything she did. They worked hard in the PTA and both showed up for the conference, even though their daughter was already doing exceptionally well.

There was only one real surprise, and she didn't realize it until the end of the day when the conferences were over. Neither parent of her little friend, accident-prone Jimmy Preston, showed up for their conference. To Chelsea, that was a real revelation. Apparently, they weren't interested in their son's schoolwork. That could explain his desperate need for attention. She shook her head sadly.

That night, she went home more tired than ever and with a lot to think about. She had made notes, and she studied them at her leisure, relating the parents mentally with each of the children. Nothing she did all year was as helpful to her as the parents' conferences. She would compare notes with the other teachers, and together they would come up with ways to help their students.

Now, she went to the closet and pulled out her overnight bag. She wouldn't need much for the brief trip to Bismarck the next day, but it had to be just right. A nice dress with matching accessories to wear to the symphony, and something casual to wear on the drive back to Stanville would be all she needed.

Packing only took a few minutes, then she had a thought. A hostess gift was a necessity, and there wasn't time to shop. She paced the floor a few minutes, thinking.

Of course, thank goodness for that weekend during spring break when she had been in one of her Martha Stewart moods.

She and Ginnie had spent an entire afternoon making pear preserves. They were beautiful and absolutely delicious. She found some tissue paper and some satin ribbon, and put the jar in a little gift bag. Perfect.

She practically fell into bed, exhausted from her day at school. What would Greg's friends be like? Had he bribed them to invite the two of them for the weekend, or what? She hoped it wouldn't be an uncomfortable situation. She didn't worry, though. After all, she herself had decided Greg McCormick was the perfect man. No need to worry.

Greg had been right about Sam, too. It all boiled down to

one thing. Chemistry, that mysterious thing that took place between two people. It hadn't been right between her and Sam. Looking back on it now, though, she realized it existed from the very first moment she met Greg. With that thought, she turned over and went to sleep.

eleven

Saturday dawned like the most perfect day she had ever encountered. Chelsea rose early, excited over her trip to Bismarck with Greg. There was not one cloud in the sky.

She dressed and ate breakfast, then there was still some time to kill before Greg picked her up, so she called Ginnie to chat a while, and tell her what good use would come of the pears they had put up.

As they talked, Ginnie said, "Greg's kind of an unusual person, isn't he? I mean, he seems like a kind of rugged man's man, and you wouldn't think he would be caught dead at a symphony, but I guess he likes that kind of music, too."

"Yes, Ginnie, he's just about the most interesting man I've ever met. In fact, he's close to perfect."

"Whoa there, pal. You sound just like a lamb that's heading for slaughter. I hate to tell you, but it's a scientific fact that there is no such thing as a perfect man. One of these days you're going to come down to earth with a real thud."

Chelsea laughed. "Oh, you just don't know him as I do. He's an exception to your so-called scientific fact."

"Well, for your sake, I hope so."

"I'd better get ready to go," Chelsea said. "Bye."

"Bye," Ginnie said. "Have fun."

Greg arrived on time, and Chelsea showed him the pears she had as a hostess gift.

"What a great idea. I'm sure Martha will be pleased. I got her some flowers." He held the door for her as she left. "Will this lock automatically?"

"Yes, it'll be fine."

"Actually, Martha won't be expecting anything. She's not that kind. She'll like the attention, though."

Once they were out on the highway, Greg tuned the radio in to the classical music station. "We'd better be getting in the mood for the symphony tonight."

Horowitz played a Chopin nocturne, and the notes floated out into the air like silver bells. "Oh, that's one of my favorites," Chelsea said. "His touch is sheer magic."

"It's a good thing I brought the car instead of the semi. You know, classical music isn't allowed in the trucks. It's a law of the road. Only Western music can be played in them."

Chelsea giggled. "What a shame those truckers have to miss this great music."

Greg nodded in agreement, but he was silent until the music ended.

"You're going to have to tell me something about these people we're visiting so I'll know what to expect," Chelsea said.

A warm smile curled Greg's lips. "They're just about the finest people you'll ever meet."

"Have you known them long?"

"Yes, longer than any of my other drivers. I knew them back in Chicago. Yes sir, the Stevensons are the kind of people who stick by you in good times and bad."

"What is he like?"

"Clem is what you'd call a man's man. He loves all kinds of sports, and he likes hunting and fishing, too. He kind of looks down his nose at tennis and golf, but give him a good baseball or football game, and he's the happiest guy on earth."

"And what about Martha? Is she a sports nut, too?"

"No, not Martha. She's a homebody. One of the few women left who still stays home and keeps house. She's real straight-laced, too. None of that live-in business for her. If she knew

I'd started dating you while you were still engaged to someone else, she would disapprove. She's a gem, though, and Clem adores her."

"I take it they're older than we are."

"Yes, considerably. I couldn't say how old. They're sort of ageless, if you know what I mean. Anyway, there's nothing to worry about. You'll like them, and you'll be very comfortable around them. I guarantee it."

"I'm sure I will if you say so."

Greg turned the music back up, and they didn't bother to keep up a running conversation. They were relaxed and happy. It was a beautiful day, and they were together. It was enough.

Chelsea was aware of the subtle fragrance of his aftershave, masculine and clean, and she took advantage of his concentration on his driving to admire his strong profile.

When she glanced out the window at the scenery from time to time, everything was perfectly flat. There was practically nothing of interest to see, except an occasional butte.

"Why did you happen to settle here in the Dakotas?" she asked.

"Not because of the scenery, if that's what you're thinking. It was on a route I knew, a good place for the trucking business, and it's remote, and I like that."

"Why do you like the idea of something remote? That's what I like least about it."

"That's because you've never lived in a big city. If you had, you would appreciate this place a lot more."

"Don't you think you will ever go back to Chicago?"

"Never," he said with finality, then he changed the subject. "When is school out?"

"The last day of May. Why do you ask?"

"I just wondered. I'm taking off on a cross-country run about that time."

This was the first she had heard about it. "You are? For how long?"

"Oh, I don't know. Could be a couple of weeks."

She was silent. Apparently he was planning his future without her. If she had entertained hopes of a wedding. . . She sighed. Better get back to reality.

They were slowing. "There's a truck stop right off the highway here. It's a good place to stop for lunch," Greg said. "Are you hungry?"

Several big semis were parked in front, and Greg drew his car up beside them.

Inside, it was a busy spot. There were only a couple of stools left at the counter, so they took them. They had to raise their voices to be heard over the jukebox which was playing a whiny, sad Western song.

The waitress was blond and buxom, with hair that had more volume than any Chelsea had seen since her last sight of Dolly Parton. The woman flung a couple of greasy menus at them, then she spied Greg and she fairly whooped.

"Howdy, Flash!" she shouted in an excited voice. "I haven't seen you in ages. Where you been keepin' yourself?"

"Hi, Ginger. Good to see you."

Ginger had spotted Chelsea and was looking her up and down with a critical eye. "I see you have a new friend," she said without enthusiasm.

"Yes, this is Chelsea Morgan. I'd like for you to meet Ginger Forrest."

"Hmmm." Ginger gave her a sympathetic look. "Well, good luck, honey. I hope you know what you're getting into."

"What'll you have?" Greg asked her.

She had been so fascinated by the Ginger character that Chelsea had forgotten to look at the menu. A quick glance told her all she needed to know. Keep it simple. "I'll have a hamburger, coleslaw, and a diet Coke."

Greg ordered the same thing, plus pie and ice cream. He looked over the assortment of pie slices under glass on the counter. "Make that cherry."

How could he eat like that and remain so lean? Chelsea noticed all the truckers were eating big pieces of pie with lots of ice cream, but some of them didn't have Greg's build. She also noticed for the first time how many of them had women traveling with them.

"Here you are, hon." Ginger set Greg's food down. "You staying over tonight?"

"Not this time. We're going on to Bismarck."

Ginger took her eyes off Greg long enough to set Chelsea's food in front of her, then she turned her attention back to Greg. "What's your hurry?"

"We have tickets for tonight."

Ginger had to pick up an order, and Chelsea gave up any thought of carrying on a pleasant conversation over the twang of the jukebox. She only ate half of her hamburger, but the coleslaw was good.

Greg turned to her. "Is something wrong with your food?"

She hated to tell him it tasted as if they had poured grease over it. She merely said, "I'm not very hungry."

When they got ready to leave, she noticed he held Ginger's hand a bit too long as they said good-bye. Back in the truck, Chelsea was silent as they drove. A depression had settled over her like a fog.

There was little to see in the way of scenery, except for Indian reservations. About the middle of the afternoon, they stopped at a small truck stop run by an unfriendly Indian. They took their drinks with them, rather than linger.

"What's his problem?" Chelsea asked.

"I guess he's still mad about Custer. This is Custer country, you know."

She laughed. "That's really holding a grudge, isn't it?"

He nodded. "Yes, but there are plenty of those people who just don't like outsiders."

They sat in the car, finishing their drinks without further conversation. Finally, Greg turned to her. "What's wrong, honey? You've been quiet ever since lunch. Did I say something that bothered you?"

"No, nothing like that." She was reluctant to tell him the truth.

"You didn't misunderstand that bit back at the truck stop, did you?"

"Maybe I did understand. Frankly, Greg, I wasn't comfortable with those people." She turned away, close to tears. "I think I made a mistake coming." She felt choked. "I'm seeing a whole new side of you. I don't know a man named Flash."

He took her shoulders and turned her toward him. "So that's it." His eyes looked deep into hers. "That's something I never talk about, but you have a right to know." He took a deep breath.

"I stopped there one night, and was just leaving the place, when I looked over to see Ginger returning from a truck parked over at the side. Suddenly there was an explosion, and it went up in flames.

"Everyone ran out yelling, 'Do something! There's a man in there!' but nobody could get near for the heat. Ginger was hysterical. 'It's my brother!' she screamed.

"I don't know how, but I got the door open and managed to pull him out." He held up his right hand, which was scarred on the palm and fingers. "Ginger's brother had a tough time of it, months in the hospital, lots of skin grafts and all that, but he's all right now.

"Ever since that time, she's called me Flash, and she practically worships me. Sometimes it's downright embarrassing."

Chelsea had tears in her eyes. "Oh, Greg, that's so like you. I should have known you couldn't change the way it appeared. Can you ever forgive me for my stupid doubts?"

She practically dissolved in his arms, and his kisses rained all over her face. "You know something? You are one complicated woman."

"No, Greg. You're the complicated one. When I try to think of you in simple terms, I'm always wrong."

As they continued their drive, Greg brought up the subject of Sam and Dolores. "I've thought a lot about their situation ever since your breakup with Sam."

"So have I. You should have seen the expression on Dolores's face when it dawned on her that she might still have a chance with Sam. Greg, she actually had tears in her eyes. It's strange. When we were going together, it never occurred to me that she had a crush on Sam."

"I saw it the first time I saw them together. Perhaps she was careful to hide her feelings around you. I've prayed about it, and I hope you have, too."

"Yes, more than once. I just hope Sam will come to realize how much he needs her."

"We'll just have to believe. It all goes back to my favorite Bible verse. 'We know that all things work together for good to them that love God.' "

Now, as they approached Bismarck the traffic became heavier, and Greg slowed his car to watch for the turnoff. Soon they drove off the interstate onto a city thoroughfare.

Like any city, Bismarck traffic was heavy in the late afternoon, and driving was slow. Finally, they turned off onto a narrower street, into a neighborhood of small brick houses.

"This looks like it," Greg said. "I'm looking for 6922." He

drove slowly down the tree-lined street, then he stopped. "Wouldn't you know it? They're standing outside watching for us."

twelve

They slowed in front of the neatest house in the neighborhood. The windows sparkled, the lawn was carefully manicured, and flowering shrubs brightened the entrance. The house didn't differ much from the neighbors' except for the flower beds that circled the front.

Chelsea observed a tall, large-boned woman with plain brownish-gray hair cut in a neat bob. Standing beside her, the man was quite tall and lean, with light, graying hair and craggy features. *He looks like an old cowboy star,* she thought.

They both broke into a grin and waved at sight of Greg's car. Now they hurried out to the curb, motioning for Greg to drive up into the driveway.

The introductions were quick, and Chelsea and Martha went in ahead, chatting comfortably already.

Clem, dressed in comfortable jeans and a plaid shirt, followed with Greg's bag, leaving him with only Chelsea's bag and the flowers to bring in.

"It doesn't look like you need these," he said, handing them to Martha.

"You know I can't get too many flowers," she said, taking the bouquet.

It was Chelsea's turn to present her pear preserves, and Martha took them graciously. "My, aren't these elegant? We'll have to try these with my biscuits tonight." She turned to Clem. "Now, isn't it nice to see a girl so domestic these days?"

Clem nodded. "I reckon Greg knows a good catch when he sees one."

Martha ushered Chelsea to her room, which turned out to be a mother-in-law room built onto the house as an after-thought. "We built this with the idea my mother would live here, but she passed away before she could move in," Martha explained. "There's even a bathroom here."

"It makes a wonderful guest room," Chelsea said.

"Yes, but we don't get much company. My brother comes up from Chicago about once a year, and Greg stops by when-ever he's out this way."

They returned to the living room, where Greg and Clem were discussing baseball. "Too bad you can't stay long enough to take in a game with me sometime," Clem said.

"Let's go in the kitchen," Martha suggested. "They're into one of their sports things. I don't know why it is two men always have to talk about sports when they get together."

She led the way back to the kitchen. "I need to check on my cooking." She opened the oven and tested the roast.

Chelsea thought she had never seen so much food. Every surface was covered with dishes, some already prepared and some in the process. There were two kinds of pies, cherry and apple, biscuits all ready to go into the oven, several kinds of vegetables, relishes, iced tea, and coffee.

"What can I do to help?"

"Oh, mercy. I don't need any help. Just sit here and tell me about yourself. How long have you known Greg?"

She thought for a moment. "Just a little over a month." Was that all? It seemed as if she had known him forever.

This amused Martha. "He's a fast worker, isn't he? All this time and him not married, and now all of a sudden he just can't do enough for you."

"Well, I wouldn't want to give you the wrong impression,"

Chelsea demurred. "We're just good friends."

"Oh now, you can't fool Martha. I saw how he looked at you, and you don't suppose he would be driving all this way and taking you to the symphony if you were just any friend." She went to the sink and started peeling potatoes.

Chelsea saw it was no use trying to play down her relationship with Greg to Martha. The woman had made up her mind this was the love affair of the century. "I will admit he is a very special person. How long have you and Clem known him?"

"Since he was a kid. You might say we watched him grow up. Clem drove for his brother in Chicago."

Martha put the potatoes on to cook and took the roast out of the oven. "I'll let this set a spell before I slice it." She slipped the other vegetables in the oven to warm. "I reckon we can put these salads on." She set out molded salads on lettuce leaves.

Chelsea took one in each hand and commenced setting them on the table in the dining room. The table was set with the best china on blue linen place mats. A centerpiece arrangement of flowers and forsythia branches from the yard echoed the bouquet Greg had brought, which was placed in a crystal vase on the buffet.

"Your table looks beautiful," Chelsea said, taking more salads. "Did you arrange those flowers?"

"Thanks. Yes, I learned that at the garden club."

Chelsea put the last of the salads on the table in the dining room. Greg and Clem were wrapped up in their ball game, and hardly noticed her.

Back in the kitchen, she helped Martha put the finishing touches on the meal. Between the two of them, they managed to get all the dishes set out on the buffet, then Martha called for the men to come in to dinner. "And I mean right now," she said. "No dawdling over that game."

They knew she meant business, so they turned off the game

and trooped into the dining room. They waited while Chelsea filled her plate, then Greg, Clem, and Martha, who insisted on being last. "I'll just get the biscuits out of the oven while you fill your plates."

Clem said the blessing as they held hands. "Bless this food, dear Lord, and the good friends who are here to share it with us."

Chelsea knew for sure she had never eaten better food. Greg made a special point of complimenting her on her pear preserves, and she saw Martha nudge Clem, in case he hadn't noticed. In fact, Martha liked them so well she asked for Chelsea's recipe. "I'd like to try them myself."

The dinner was a warm, cozy affair, with Chelsea feeling quite comfortable with these old friends. They talked of their days in Chicago and asked lots of questions about Chelsea's teaching job.

"She's one of the best teachers in the school," Greg bragged, and Chelsea caught a knowing glance between Martha and Clem.

"I don't know about that," Chelsea said modestly, "but I do love my work."

She helped Martha clear off the table and serve the dessert. They had their choice of pies, both delicious. Martha poured coffee, and they lingered to talk more after they finished eating.

Even though dinner had been early, they finally realized they would have to hurry to make the concert on time. Martha insisted it would be no trouble to put the dishes in the dishwasher and refused Chelsea's offer to do them after the concert.

Chelsea dressed hurriedly, wearing her best red silk dress and a light matching jacket. Greg's eyes lit up at the sight of her.

"I haven't seen that. You'll be the prettiest woman there."

Martha grinned. "Yes, indeed. You'll be proud of her tonight, Greg."

The couple chatted as they drove to the concert hall.

"You were right, Greg. I love Martha and Clem. They couldn't be nicer."

"Yes, I knew you would. You'll have to make allowances, though. They seem to have the idea we're the romance of the century. I hope they don't embarrass you."

She laughed. "So you noticed, too. I hate to disappoint them. I tried to tell Martha we hadn't known each other very long, but it didn't seem to make any difference."

He glanced over at her. "You do look smashing tonight."

"Thanks. You do, too. I hardly ever see you in a suit and tie. Do you realize that?"

"No. I'm just a casual sort of guy."

"Aren't you excited about the concert? I don't get to attend many, you know."

"Don't expect too much. This is a good orchestra, but it isn't great. They have their weaknesses, but we're lucky to have one at all up here. This is hardly a cultural center."

He drove into the parking garage, and they made their way slowly into the auditorium in the midst of the well-dressed throng. Chelsea followed the usher down to excellent center seats.

"What wonderful seats," she said, as they made themselves comfortable.

There was just time to glance over the program before the lights dimmed, and a hush fell over the audience as the concertmaster, then the conductor, walked briskly to the center of the stage. They were welcomed with applause, and after a gracious bow to the audience, the conductor raised his baton as an indication for the audience to stand. A lively rendition of "The Star Spangled Banner" followed.

After that, they settled back to enjoy the music.

The star of the evening was the winner of a prestigious New York piano competition, a graduate of the Moscow Conservatory of Music. He played the Mozart C-Minor Concerto with great feeling.

Chelsea relaxed and let the music flow over her, oblivious to everything else. The young man played brilliantly, from the beginning with its sonorous tones, through all three movements.

Once he finished, the audience applauded enthusiastically, bringing him out again and again for curtain calls. A brief encore of a Russian folk song brought still more applause. Finally, the lights came on for intermission, and Chelsea and Greg went out for a cold drink.

Greg spoke first, handing her a soft drink. "Well, what do you think? Was he that good?"

"I thought so. I'll bet they don't have artists of that caliber very often."

"No, I think this young man was very special. I'm no judge of classical music, but I enjoyed it very much."

"So did I. That particular concerto is one of my favorites." She glanced at her program. The remainder of the program would consist of a composition by Mahler, then it would end with the familiar New World Symphony.

They finished their drinks as the lights blinked, then returned to their seats. Without the exciting performance of the young pianist, the rest of the evening was even more relaxing. Chelsea found her mind wandering as her senses were engulfed in the music. She was much more conscious of Greg sitting beside her.

Once, during the Mahler, she glanced over at him, and he reached for her hand. With their fingers entwined, the music became even more personal to them. A warmth flooded over her as he squeezed her hand, and she wondered if he felt the same way.

Chelsea appreciated the fact that Greg didn't turn on the radio during their trip back from the concert. It would have broken the spell of the music. Instead, they carried on a low-key conversation, and at his urging, she sat very close to him.

Greg asked her a question she had often wondered about. "What would you have been if you hadn't decided to be a teacher?"

"An artist," she said without hesitation, "but I doubt that I could have made a living at it. I suppose I might have been more practical. Maybe I would have become a librarian, like Ginnie. That has a certain appeal."

"Mmmm, I can see you doing that, but I think you should be painting now, if only for a hobby."

"I know. It's just so hard to find the time." Then she asked him the same question.

"Me? I'd have been a baseball player."

"Were you good at it as a kid?"

"You bet. I could slam that ball farther than any of the neighborhood boys."

She gave him an admiring glance. "You never cease to amaze me. I can see right now I'm going to have to brush up on my baseball. I'm practically a sports illiterate," she admitted.

"Why not let me teach you? I'd like that." He turned the car into the driveway of Clem and Martha's house.

Before she made a move to get out of the car, Greg reached for her and pulled her next to him. "I've been wanting to do this all evening," he said as he leaned down to kiss her.

This time, his kiss was warm and slow, and she felt his warmth beneath her light jacket.

She returned his kiss, circling his neck with her arms, her

fingers entwined in his curly black hair. The pounding of her heart was so loud she felt sure he could hear it.

His lips moved over her face, brushing it with soft little kisses, then down to the soft curve of her neck.

Her breath came in little gasps as she spoke. "Oh, Greg," she sighed, "I hate to leave, but Clem and Martha will be wondering what we're doing out here."

He grumbled. "I suppose so." They kissed once more, this time as a sort of passionate finale; then they went into the house, which was dark, except for a light in the utility room at the back door. They could imagine Clem and Martha lying in the dark, wide awake, waiting for them to settle down.

Greg left her at the door to her room after one last quick kiss. "Good night. I'll see you in the morning." She left her door open with the light on until he went down the hall and turned on the light in his room.

The next morning she was awakened quite early by the sound of Martha fixing breakfast in the kitchen nearby. She lay in bed a while, remembering Greg's kisses and the way they had made her feel. Now that her engagement was off, he wasn't wasting any time.

After a quick shower, she dressed and went into the kitchen. Martha turned and greeted her. "Good morning. I hope you slept well."

"Yes, that's a very comfortable bed. What can I do to help?"

"Oh, it's all ready, honey. Just help yourself to some juice and coffee while I finish these hash browns."

The kitchen table was all set, and Chelsea knew there would be biscuits and gravy and eggs and hash browns even before she saw it all on the back of the stove. She wondered how Martha and Clem stayed so lean. Probably lots of hard work, she guessed.

"All right," Martha said. "I believe it's ready." She stepped to the door and called the men. "Clem, you and Greg get in here right now. Breakfast is ready." Her tone held an unmistakable air of authority.

Martha directed the seating arrangement, and they took their places at once. She set the warm plates of food before them and poured hot coffee.

"I could get used to this kind of breakfast real easily," Greg said.

Chelsea smiled at him. "All you have to do is convince some woman she should get up an hour early to cook all this."

Martha chuckled. "I reckon your generation goes in more for fast foods. Well, cooking and housekeeping is all I have to do, and I love every minute of it."

Greg turned to her with a mischievous grin. "Martha, honey, if anything ever happens to Clem, I want to be first on the list to take his place."

Martha howled at that. "You've got it, hon, and don't you forget."

Clem had been watching them with quiet amusement. Now he changed the subject. "How was the concert last night?"

"Wonderful, Clem," Greg replied. "There's a whole world of great music out there you've never experienced. You ought to try it sometime. You might like it."

"Not unless they can come up with some decent Western music."

Martha gave him a loving pat. "That's all right, hon. You have enough going on now to keep you contented. There aren't enough hours in the day now for him to enjoy all his sports and hobbies."

Martha passed hot biscuits around every few minutes and kept the coffee mugs filled with steaming coffee. After breakfast, there was the paper to look through, and Clem had to take Greg out to the garage to show him his new hunting rifle.

"I just wish Greg lived here," Martha said, once they were out of sight. "I can't tell you how Clem enjoys his company."

"Yes, and Greg is equally fond of both of you. It's been such a pleasure for me to get to know you."

"Can't you stay for church? We have a fine little neighborhood church just a couple of blocks away. There's just time to clear these dishes out and change our clothes."

"I'd love to, if it's all right with Greg."

Martha went to the door and called to Clem. "Time to get ready for church."

The men walked in slowly, chatting all the while. Greg agreed that he would like to visit Clem and Martha's church. "You don't mind if we have to drive a bit after dark, do you, honey?"

"Not at all."

They changed quickly, and Martha insisted she would clean up the kitchen after church. "It will keep me from that lonely feeling you get when someone you love leaves."

The parking lot was already full, and they parked on the street. "We could have walked," Clem observed, "but I know you ladies don't like to walk in heels."

Clem and Martha greeted friends as they went in, with quick introductions of Chelsea and Greg. The organ started playing just as they took their seats. Martha nudged Chelsea. "You'll love our minister. He's the best."

Their services followed the same format as the church in New Mill. When the minister came in, Chelsea was surprised that he was so young. He was both confident and natural, and she listened carefully to his sermon.

"The Lord is my light and my salvation; whom shall I fear? the Lord is the strength of my life; of whom shall I be afraid?"

It was a strong sermon, meant to counteract the worst that could befall anyone. It couldn't have been more uplifting, and when they left, all four of them were uncharacteristically silent, thinking of his words.

Finally, Greg spoke first. "You have a great minister there. I hope your congregation appreciates him."

"Oh, you can be sure we do," they assured him.

Back home, it was time to say good-bye. Greg put their bags in the car, then came back to where they waited on the porch. "I can't tell you how much we've enjoyed this weekend," he said. He gave Martha a big kiss. "Especially your good food, Martha. Thanks for everything."

Chelsea repeated her thanks, taking Martha's hand in a warm gesture.

Martha and Clem stood outside and watched as Greg backed the car out of the driveway. The couple waved until the car was out of sight.

"What dear people," Chelsea said. "It really was a wonderful weekend."

"Yes," he agreed. "Clem and Martha are the only part of my life back in Chicago, besides my family, that I didn't leave behind when I moved here. I couldn't leave them out of my life."

"I'm glad, and I think you mean as much to them as they do to you."

"There's something about starting a new life that's exhilarating," he said. "I speak from experience." He stared at the road in silence for a while as he drove. Finally, he spoke again. "You're starting a new life, too."

"Yes. I hadn't thought of it that way, but I am." She, too, became silent as she thought of her new life. Sam was no longer the center of her life. She was completely on her own now. Free to do as she pleased.

"You know, I like my new freedom."

He reached over and patted her on the shoulder. "Sure you

do." There was admiration in his voice. "You're too independent to want it any other way."

Greg played his Horowitz tape most of the way back, and it seemed to Chelsea it was the most thrilling music she had ever heard. He had the good sense not to try to carry on a conversation while she was listening to it, and for that she respected him even more. It was just one more thing that convinced her he was the perfect man.

Ha! she thought, remembering Ginnie's cynical observation. *You're wrong, Ginnie. Wrong, wrong, wrong. There is such a thing as a perfect man, and I've found him!*

thirteen

Phyllis was the center of attention in the teachers' lounge. "Now, don't tell a soul," she said, and her voice was very low, "but you'll never guess who I went to the movies with Saturday night."

The four teachers standing around her breathed the answer in an ecstacy of romantic delight. "Oh, Phyllis! You and Mr. Garner!"

"None other." She tossed her blond hair and looked ever so pleased with herself. "This is just between us," she cautioned, as if she didn't know everyone in Stanville would hear about it by this evening.

Chelsea mopped her lips with her napkin, having choked on her coffee. "I have to run," she said. "I'll see you at lunch."

She hurried down the hall to Thomas Garner's office and tapped on the door.

He greeted her with a big smile and a warm "hello." Mentally, Chelsea tried to picture him as an intellectual football player, but she still couldn't see it. *Just one of Ginnie's fantasies,* she supposed.

"I know you're busy, but I wanted to ask if you could come to a little dinner party I'm having Saturday night. I've invited a friend I go with and a woman I think you would like to meet because you have similar interests."

I had to put it that way, she reasoned. *If I had just invited him without any explanation, he might have asked if he could bring Phyllis.*

He accepted with pleasure, and she relaxed. Then her

136

thoughts turned to school. As the weather grew warmer, the children could play outside more, thus making her job easier. They could work off some of their energy without doing it in the classroom.

That night, before she could call Greg to invite him to her party, the phone rang and it was Greg. His words were triumphant. "Congratulations, you great little matchmaker! Sam and Dolores were married in the minister's private office after church Sunday night."

"Praise the Lord! How did you find out?"

"I went by Sam's office to leave some work, and it was locked. There was a note on the door which said 'Closed. Will return next Monday.' "

"That could mean anything. How did you find out they were married?"

"I suspected that was what happened, but I had to know for sure, so I called the minister. He confirmed that he had married them after church Sunday evening. He said Sam had wanted them to elope, but Dolores insisted she didn't want to have anyone but her pastor perform the ceremony. It was very hush-hush, but I assured him I would keep it confidential until they could make their own announcement."

"Oh, that makes me feel so much better. I promise I won't breathe a word to anyone. I knew Sam was a fast worker, but this really beats all."

"I wasn't sure it would work, but I'm glad we made the try."

"Yes, I was just getting ready to call you. I'm having our new principal and Ginnie over for a little dinner Saturday night. Could you come?"

"Sure. I'd love to. What time?"

"About seven. See you then."

As the end of school approached, Ginnie found herself thinking more and more about Greg's two-week cross-country drive. That wasn't such a long time, but she knew it would seem endless to her, waiting at home.

The rest of her spare time that week was taken up with party preparations. She decided to make it a Mexican dinner and planned everything to carry out that theme.

The morning of the party, she checked the weather. . .perfect. That was a good sign. She worked hard all day, cleaning and cooking, interrupted only by a long-distance phone call from her mother. Chelsea tried to talk her into coming for a week, but did manage to convince her she could be spared for a weekend, long enough to meet Greg. They said good-bye, until next weekend.

By 6:30 that evening, the apartment was spotless, the food was ready to go into the oven, and the before-dinner appetizers were ready to serve.

Ginnie was the first to arrive, carrying her pecan pie. "I hope this is good. I slaved over it all morning. I even made my own crust."

Chelsea took it to the kitchen, admiring it extravagantly. She set it on the counter, then hurried to answer the doorbell. Greg stood there, wearing his jeans and a dark blue casual shirt, looking so good she could hardly find the words to greet him.

She invited him in and took the flowers he held out to her. "How did you know? They match my decor perfectly." He and Ginnie chatted while she went to the kitchen to pour little glasses of tomato juice and put them and some cheese on a tray.

Now Thomas was at the door, and Chelsea invited him in and made introductions all around.

Thomas stared at Ginnie with an astonished expression. "Why, you're the librarian!" He thrust out his hand. "This is a real coincidence. I've been wanting to meet you."

As far as Chelsea was concerned, that made the evening,

and from there it could only be a success. They sat and chatted comfortably, enjoying their appetizers, talking of the books they had read and the latest best-sellers they hadn't yet read.

When they went in to dinner, there were oohs and aahs over her colorful table, set with bright Mexican place mats and a centerpiece of huge paper flowers she had found at a charity bazaar. Greg's flowers were perfect on the counter dividing the dining room and the kitchen.

Chelsea felt she had never had a more successful party. The conversation was good, and the food was, too. At least, the men took seconds, which was a good sign.

Greg insisted on helping her clear up the dishes after the others had left. "I like Thomas," he said. "I hope we can see more of him. How do you think Ginnie liked him?"

She laughed. "Actually, he has been in the library quite a few times, and she had thought he was very attractive. I just thought he should meet someone besides schoolteachers, since he was new in town."

"It was nice of you to see that he and Ginnie had a chance to meet under such good circumstances."

"I just had a hunch they might like each other, and the way it worked out, I believe I was right."

"It seems to have worked in their case, but I should think it would be risky sometimes."

"Yes. I wouldn't try it unless I thought it had a good chance of succeeding."

"Sometimes things just work out when you let nature take its course, like when I found you standing by your stalled car."

"Yes, but you'll have to admit cases like that are pretty rare. I'm still not sure how we ever managed to get together."

"Neither am I, but I'm glad. Maybe it was just part of God's plan."

"I think Sam and Dolores were the riskiest bit of match-making I ever tried."

"I know. That was a desperation move, and we were lucky that time. It did work, and I wouldn't have given it even fifty-fifty odds."

They continued working until all the dishes were put up, and the dishwasher was started. "I guess I'd better run along now," Greg said, hanging up his dish towel.

"Thanks for helping." Chelsea smoothed lotion on her hands. "Mother will be here next weekend, and I would love for you to meet her."

"I'd like that."

"Good. I'll call and let you know what time." She walked to the door with him.

"Thanks for everything. It was a great party." He took her in his arms and kissed her over and over. "You're quite a gal," he said admiringly, and his eyes glowed with a deep emotion.

"Good night," she said, and watched as he strode down the hall and out of sight. A deep sigh escaped from her throat as she closed the door and locked it.

❧

On Monday, she returned to school feeling as if she had been away a week instead of merely a weekend. The children were unusually boisterous because they were energized by the beautiful spring weather. She didn't try too hard to hold them down. She just tried not to let it bother her.

After school, she was relieved to be rid of the responsibility for a while. She sighed. Some days were harder than others, but even on the tough days, she loved her work.

She had already made the decision to transfer to the New Mill school, and she had settled in her mind that she would miss the Stanville school. She still intended to go through with the move, even though her wedding with Sam was off. It was a step up to a bigger school, an increase in pay; and, she reasoned, there were all new children in her class every year anyway.

She dropped by the library on the way home. Ginnie was at the desk, checking out a book for a patron. Finally, she looked up. "Guess who called a while ago?"

"Not Thomas." Chelsea's eyed sparkled at the prospect.

"None other. Your party did the job. He asked me for a date next Saturday night. I've been dying to tell you."

"How wonderful. I was so impressed with him at the party. He's even more fun when he gets away from school and loosens up."

"I think so, too, and he even got along well with Greg." Chelsea nodded. "You never know how people will interact with each other. Greg is a big-city fellow and I'm a small-town girl. He grew up in Chicago where his family still lives, and I grew up in Bedford where my mother still lives. You might think we wouldn't get along so well, but we're just perfect for each other.

"Yes, I was afraid he and Thomas wouldn't have anything in common, but they seemed to fit right in. I hope we can double-date soon."

"So do I. Have you talked to Greg since last night?"

"Yes, he called earlier. He's coming to dinner Saturday to meet my mother, who is coming up for a visit. I'm to pick her up at the airport after school Friday."

"That's wonderful. You haven't seen her in quite a while, have you?"

"No, and I'm really looking forward to her visit."

"Of course you are. Has she ever met Greg?"

"No. I hope she'll like him."

"I'm sure she will."

"Maybe not. After all, she thought Sam was the greatest

thing that ever lived, and she thought I was crazy to break up with him."

"Don't worry. Once she gets to know Greg, she will change her mind."

"I hope so. I haven't visited home in quite a while and I'm anxious for things to go well. I honestly wish we lived closer. You know, I envy you living here in the same town with your mother."

"Yes, I'm lucky. Sometimes we get on each other's nerves, and I have to remind myself how much I'd miss her if she moved away, but I guess everyone feels that way occasionally."

"Sure. It's normal. I have to run now," Chelsea said. "I have a million things to do, getting ready for Mother's visit."

Chelsea's mother, Hope Morgan, was a taller, thinner version of her daughter, and Chelsea was dismayed to see she had lost weight. They hugged as soon as Hope got off the plane. Chelsea took her carry-on bag. "Is this all you brought?"

"Yes, it's plenty for a weekend." They made their way to the car, and Chelsea started telling her about Greg immediately.

"I can't wait for you to meet him. He's one of the most decent people you'll ever meet. He's honest, straightforward, and intelligent."

"Sounds like Abraham Lincoln. Does he have any money?"

"Oh, Mother, what a thing to say! He has a good business. I'd say he's quite comfortably situated. He is coming for dinner tomorrow night. I just know you're going to like him."

Chelsea had prepared a delicious chicken salad, which was one of her mother's favorites, and they caught up on the latest family news over dinner.

"How's Aunt Joanne?"

"She's holding her own, I'm glad to say. Maybe your prayer circle is helping. I would have been up to see you sooner, but I need to spend as much time with her as I can."

"I understand. Cancer is so terrible. Be sure to give her my love."

"I will."

They watched TV for a while after dinner, then Hope excused herself. "I had better get to bed. You know, traveling is so tiring."

Chelsea kissed her good night. "I'll see you in the morning. Sleep as late as you want to."

The alarm went off early the next morning, and Chelsea busied herself with dinner preparations. She tried not to feel nervous, but she had to admit she was feeling a bit apprehensive that Greg wouldn't be able to overcome her mother's prejudice in favor of Sam.

Her mother didn't sleep very late, so once she ate a light breakfast, she was able to help Chelsea with the dinner preparations.

They worked a good part of the day, taking time off to eat a sandwich for lunch. Hope insisted she didn't want much. "I'm saving for tonight. It looks like you're going all out. I hope this young man is worth the effort."

"Oh, he is. You'll see."

By the appointed time, the apartment was spick-and-span, the food was ready, and Chelsea and her mother looked as if they hadn't lifted a finger all day.

When the doorbell rang, Chelsea hurried to open it. Greg was wearing a coat and tie, looking ever so sophisticated and handsome. She couldn't resist a glance at her mother. There was a spark of interest in her eyes. If she had been expecting Greg to look like a truck driver, this must be quite a surprise.

Chelsea accepted the flowers he handed her with thanks, then introduced him to her mother.

Greg took Hope's hand in his. "I'm delighted, Mrs. Morgan.

It's easy to see where Chelsea gets her looks."

Mrs. Morgan smiled at him. "Call me Hope. I must say, you're nothing like the man I was expecting to meet."

From that moment on, the evening was a complete success. They chatted about Chelsea's early years, then on to Greg's school days. "Did you go to school in Chicago?" Hope asked.

"Yes, I attended University of Chicago for a couple of years, then went on to Harvard to finish. I got my degree in business administration."

"Oh, my. Chelsea didn't tell me that you were a Harvard graduate."

There was no doubt in Chelsea's mind, Greg had won over her mother. She relaxed and enjoyed her dinner party.

The evening ended on a pleasant note, with Greg telling Mrs. Morgan how delightful it had been meeting her. Chelsea saw him to the door, and he gave her a light kiss. "Thanks. I enjoyed the evening, and your mother is charming."

On Sunday evening, Chelsea took her mother to the airport and kissed her good-bye. They had gone to church together that morning and had prayed for her Aunt Joanne.

After church, they had gone for brunch at Barcarolle. Their conversation had centered around Greg, and Chelsea was amused at her mother's quick turnaround.

"You know, dear, I do believe I like Greg better than Sam. Not that I didn't like Sam, but Greg is just so. . .you know, rugged and smooth at the same time. It's hard to describe. You're not going to let this one get away, are you?"

"Let's just say I hope not. You have to realize we haven't known each other long, and he hasn't asked me to marry him. I'm just hoping for the best."

Chelsea stayed with her mother until she boarded her plane, then she drove home, taking time to enjoy the late spring wild-flowers by the side of the road. The sky was blue and cloudless, and a strong breeze rippled the tall grass in the fields.

The phone was ringing when she walked into her apartment. She tossed her purse on a chair and hurried to answer it.

Greg's voice sounded strong and upbeat. "Hi. Hope I didn't interrupt anything."

"Not at all. I just returned from taking Mother to the airport. As you might have guessed, you made quite a hit with her."

"Glad to hear it. I liked her, too. I just called to let you know I enjoyed your dinner and meeting your mother. She's charming."

"Thanks. Just one more weekend until the end of school."

"So there is. How about trying some of my cooking next weekend?"

"You cook, too?"

"I charcoal things, if you want to call that cooking."

"Sounds good. Can I bring something?"

"No need. I'll pick you up about 6:30."

"I can drive over. You don't need to do that."

"No, I insist. Actually I'm going to be over that way anyway, but I don't trust you out on the highway. No telling who would pick you up in case you had car trouble."

She laughed. "It could lead to all sorts of things. Okay, I'll be looking for you."

fourteen

The next week seemed endless. The talk in the teachers' lounge was of survival until the final day. On Friday, a fight broke out in Chelsea's class. One of the boys missed some change from his locker and accused another boy of taking it. There were hot words between them, and before she could intervene, they were rolling around on the floor, pummeling each other.

By the time she could break it up, she was in a panicky cold sweat, remembering the fight that caused Mr. Culpepper's heart attack.

At last, the week was over, and late Saturday Greg showed up for their date just as Chelsea finished brushing her hair. She had dressed casually in jeans and a red knit shirt. "How about a little lemonade before we start back to New Mill?"

"I'd like that. It's getting pretty warm out there. I believe we're going to have an early summer."

Chelsea poured lemonade into two frosty glasses. "I hope so. Here's to the end of school. It's almost over." She told him about the fight.

Greg chuckled. "Boys will be boys. I had my share of fights when I was their age."

"I suppose so, but it doesn't make my job any easier."

"What you need is a good home-cooked meal." He finished his lemonade. "Shall we get going?"

"I'm ready. Do I dare ask what you're planning to cook tonight?"

"I'm doing some grilled Cajun chicken. It's something I

picked up in New Orleans."

"You're full of surprises. I was half expecting steak, even though I never eat it."

"That's why I'm not having it." He opened the car door for her, and she reached back and fastened her seat belt.

Once they were out on the highway, Greg asked her if she had ever been to New Orleans.

"No, it's on my list of places I want to see."

"You'll love it. It's one of my favorite cities. I've been there on business a number of times."

They talked of travel as they drove. Chelsea realized how limited her traveling had been and vowed to make up for it someday. She would try to see a new place each summer on her vacation.

Greg's house was comfortable, but modest. "I'm renting this right now," he explained. "When the time is right, I want to build my dream home. I already have a beautiful lot on the edge of town. I'll show you sometime."

They went out to the patio, where Greg started the fire in his grill. The weather was still warm, and a soft breeze feathered Chelsea's hair. The moonlight was so bright, they didn't even need a light. Chelsea sighed contentedly. "It would be a shame to spend this gorgeous night cooped up inside, wouldn't it? Even the stars seem closer tonight."

Greg put his arm around her shoulders and squeezed her affectionately. "You know, honey, everything seems more perfect than usual tonight. In fact, I feel like an eighteen-year-old out on a big date."

She smiled. "I wish I had known you then. I'll bet you were something."

"Not really. Just an ordinary shy kid."

A table was set on the patio, and Greg offered her some iced tea and assorted appetizers of nuts, pretzels, and crackers.

"Can I do anything to help?"

"No, thanks. I have everything ready to go."

All through the evening, Chelsea kept hoping Greg would get an idea from Dolores and Sam's sudden wedding, but there was nothing in the conversation to indicate any such thought had entered his mind.

The meal started with steaming cups of gumbo, which he brought out from the kitchen, where it had been warming on the back of the stove. He generously shook hot sauce on his. "Don't you want some of this? It really improves the flavor."

"Maybe just a tiny bit." She could never understand why people would want to make their mouths burn. She had to admit, though, it did go well in the gumbo.

Soon the chicken was done, and Greg filled their plates with chicken breasts, risotto heated in foil on the back of the grill, and a green salad from a frosty salad bowl on the table. Buttered French bread was also heated on the grill, and he served that in a basket.

This meal was far and away better than Chelsea had been expecting. "I think you should open a restaurant. This is great."

"Somehow I don't think Cajun will ever be big in Nebraska. In fact, I was a little worried that you might not go for it tonight."

She reassured him. "Don't be silly. I love it."

The ice cream he brought out for dessert was not home-made, but it was delicious, and the cooling texture went well after the hot meal.

They talked of the places he would go on his cross-country trip, which he planned in a couple of weeks. The first stop would be a little town called Valentine, Nebraska. He had friends there. Next he would go to Cheyenne, Wyoming, where he would spend the night. Wyoming was beautiful, rugged country. Nature at its best. The next morning, he would head for Salt Lake City. He had an old college friend there, he explained.

His descriptions were so realistic, Chelsea could almost see these places. "Have you ever been to the Grand Canyon?" he asked.

"No, I'm just realizing how little I've traveled." She couldn't tell him how much she would like to go on a trip like that with him. It couldn't be, unless he asked her to marry him, and it didn't look as if that was going to happen.

By the time Greg brought her home, Chelsea was sure this would go down in her memory as one of the best evenings she had ever spent.

Even his good-night kiss held a special magic. Perhaps it was the spell of the moonlight, but they clung to each other for ever so long. Neither of them wanted to spoil the beauty of the moment.

When at last they entered her apartment building, they were like two sleepwalkers in the midst of a dream. Chelsea unlocked her door, slowly turned and melted into Greg's arms for one last warm, tender kiss. Their good-byes were whispered against their cheeks.

Monday was the last day of school. Common sense would have told the school officials to let school out on the previous Friday; however, they had lost an extra snow day that year, so it had to be made up.

The children's thoughts were on everything but schoolwork. Every teacher knew better than to expect anyone to learn anything right at the end of school. Just get through the day. Thank goodness the weather was still good and the students could be turned loose on the playground.

When the last recess was reached, there was already a feeling of relaxation. They were actually going to make it. Chelsea stood on the playground next to the jungle gym, on recess duty for the last time this school year.

Suddenly she turned at the sound of a blood-curdling Tarzan yell. Jimmy Preston stood on the top, beating his chest. All eyes were on him, riveted by the danger of his position. How did he get up there? As they watched, his yell turned to a scream when he lost his balance and came hurtling down.

Chelsea managed to leap the short distance to break his fall. *Lord, help me!* she prayed as she held out her arms to catch him, then everything went black.

ße

A strange jiggling motion was the first thing Chelsea was aware of. She opened her eyes to see that she was on a stretcher being taken into the hospital. "What happened? Where am I?"

Thomas Garner walked along beside her. "You had an accident. Just relax. Don't try to talk."

Her thoughts were chaotic. She tried to remember. . .Jimmy Preston. . . "Jimmy? Is he. . .?"

"Don't worry. Thanks to you, he's okay. You broke his fall, but you hit your head on the iron bar supporting the jungle gym."

"Oh, thank God!" Chelsea faded from consciousness again.

The next time she awoke, she was settled snugly in a hospital bed. A nurse stood over her, changing the bandage on her head. "Good. You're awake. How do you feel?"

"Groggy. What are you doing?"

"You had quite a whack on the head. You've had a concussion. The doctor says you need to stay quiet for a while."

Chelsea reached up to feel her head, and discovered a bandage covering a good part of it. "Ugh. I must look like Frankenstein's monster."

"Do you feel like seeing a visitor?"

"Who is it?"

"A young woman who says she's a friend of yours. I believe she said her name was Ginnie something."

"Oh, yes. Please let me see her."

"Just for a few minutes." The nurse left and Ginnie came in, looking very serious.

"Oh, Chelsea, you poor thing. Thomas called me, and I came right over. How do you feel?"

"Oh, it's nothing. Just a slight concussion. I'll be out of here before you know it. Can you tell me if Jimmy Preston is okay? He could have been killed. What a crazy kid."

"Thomas left as soon as I got here. He said you saved that little boy's life."

"I wonder how long they're going to keep me here. I need to get out."

"Thomas talked to the doctor, and he said he would know more tomorrow. He definitely wants to keep you overnight."

The nurse came in and told Ginnie she would have to leave so the patient could rest. Ginnie squeezed her hand. "Take it easy. I'll keep in touch."

Chelsea drifted off to sleep immediately. When she awoke almost an hour later, the doctor was checking her blood pressure. "Hello. I'm Dr. Cabot. How do you feel?"

"Okay. When can I get out of here?"

"You patients are all alike. We pamper you and make you comfortable, and all you can think of is getting out." He grinned. "You're going to be fine. I just need to monitor you tonight. I'll probably sign you out tomorrow." He hurried out on his rounds to check his next patient.

The nurse stuck her head in the door. "Do you feel up to seeing another visitor?"

"Yes, I'm doing fine."

Greg appeared at the door, and Chelsea heard the nurse tell

him not to stay too long. He hurried to her side, his eyes dark with worry.

"Chelsea!" He kissed her. "You poor darling. I know just how you feel."

"Yes, it's my turn to have a concussion now. Did you drive all the way over here just to see me?"

"Of course. Just as soon as Ginnie called me."

"You must have a million things to do. Aren't you leaving on your cross-country tour tomorrow?"

"Not now. Not without you. Oh, Chelsea, I've been such a fool. I didn't want to rush you the way Sam did. I know now that was a big mistake. I can't go anywhere without you."

He swallowed hard. "I nearly died when I heard about your accident. What if I had waited too long? Oh, Chelsea, I love you so much." His face was close to hers, and he kissed her again ever so tenderly. "Will you marry me, darling?"

The nurse was at the door. "I'm sorry, sir. It's time to leave."

"Yes! Oh, Greg, yes, yes, yes!"

❧

It was 11:00 the following morning when Greg appeared once more to check her out. "The doctor says you will be fine. I'm taking you home."

Chelsea gazed at him, still under the spell of the dream she had had during the night when he had asked her to marry him. "You came all the way over here again just to take me home?"

"I wanted to see for myself how you were."

"Well, you needn't worry. I feel fine."

Greg's smile was warm. "Good. I have something for you when we get to your apartment."

The nurse insisted on wheeling her out to the entrance, even though Chelsea insisted she felt well enough to walk.

Greg brought his car to the door and saw that she was settled in the front seat beside him.

"You don't need to treat me like an invalid," she assured him. "I feel fine."

"Yes, I know exactly how you feel. If you'll remember, I thought the same thing, but I really wasn't okay."

She smiled. How well she remembered.

They pulled up into the driveway of her apartment building, and Greg put his hand under her arm as they walked in. He insisted that she should lie on the sofa, while he fixed her a bowl of soup. "I still remember how good that soup you made for me tasted."

She relaxed completely. How good it felt to be back in her own apartment after a night in the hospital. Greg didn't need to wait on her. She sat up, certain she could make it into the kitchen. Sure, she felt a little wobbly, but that was to be expected.

He had just started in to tell her the soup was ready, when she grabbed a chair in the dinette. "I'll just sit here. No need to eat in there."

He gave her a sharp look. "I think you'd better take it easy. Maybe this will make you feel better." He placed a steaming bowl of tomato soup in front of her. "I think I'll join you. This looks pretty good." He sat across from her.

Chelsea looked at him with a curious smile. "I thought you said you had something for me."

"It's by your plate."

She had expected a bouquet of flowers, but there was nothing but. . . "Oh. . ." she gasped at the sight of a ring box.

He came around to her side. "Try it on."

She opened the box and stared at the brilliant diamond ring, dazzled. "Then it wasn't a dream?"

"What do you mean?"

"I thought I had dreamed you asked me to marry you."

Greg smiled and gently placed the ring on her finger.

"That was no dream."

She rose and kissed him. "Oh, Greg. I'm so happy. You'll never know what this means to me." She kissed him again and held her hand out to admire her ring. "It's the most beautiful ring I've ever seen."

"Sit down and eat your soup before it gets cold. You need it."

She felt her strength return as she ate. "I can't wait to tell Ginnie. She'll be thrilled."

"She called me last night to inquire about you, and she said she wanted to have us over this weekend if you're feeling up to it. I expect you'll hear from her soon."

"Oh, really? I guess she is going to have that party she's been wanting to have for Thomas. It would be fun to spring our news on them at the party, wouldn't it?"

"Yes, if you feel well enough to go."

"Oh, I'm sure I will."

After their little lunch, Greg insisted on cleaning up, then he said he needed to get back to the office.

Chelsea went back to her bedroom for a nap and didn't wake up until Ginnie called to see if she could stop by to see her.

"Sure, I'm fine," Chelsea insisted. She lovingly placed her ring in its box and went into the living room to wait for Ginnie.

About thirty minutes later, Ginnie arrived and handed Chelsea a lovely bouquet of flowers. "How are you feeling?"

She took the flowers. "Thanks. These are lovely. I feel fine. It's good to be back home. Greg checked me out of the hospital and fixed me some lunch."

"He's so attentive." Ginnie took the flowers. "Here, let me go put these in a vase."

"Thanks. Look on the top right-hand shelf."

Ginnie returned soon with the flowers which she placed on the coffee table.

"They are beautiful. You didn't need to do that."

"Well, I wanted to." She sat across from Chelsea. "I'm thinking of having a very casual little dinner party Saturday night. Do you think you'll be feeling well enough to come?"

"I'm sure I will. What can I bring?"

"Nothing. Just enjoy being an invalid for a few days. You don't get a chance to be pampered very often. I called your mother after I had talked to the doctor, and he assured me it wasn't anything critical. You might give her a ring so she won't worry."

"Yes, I'll do that."

Ginnie rose. "Is there anything I can get for you? Do you have groceries?"

"Yes, I'll be fine. I'll just heat a TV dinner tonight. Thanks for the flowers."

"You're welcome. Don't bother to see me out. I'll see you Saturday. Call me if you need anything."

"Okay. 'Bye."

During the next few days, Chelsea gradually regained her strength. She had reassured her mother with a lengthy telephone call, and Mrs. Morgan had been overjoyed to hear the news that Greg had asked her daughter to marry him. She had millions of questions about the plans, none of which Chelsea could answer. "We'll settle all that as soon as possible, and you'll be the first to know," Chelsea told her.

On Saturday, Greg picked her up to take her to Ginnie's party.

"This is going to be such fun," Chelsea said. "I can't wait to see Ginnie's face when she sees this ring."

Ginnie took advantage of the nice weather to charcoal some hamburgers on the balcony outside her apartment. She bought some potato salad and coleslaw from the deli, and with one of her famous pecan pies, it turned out to be a very satisfying meal.

Of course, the high point of the evening was when Ginnie first noticed Chelsea's ring. Ever since she arrived, Chelsea had been flaunting it, holding her hand up to her face, and in general showing it off in every possible exaggerated gesture.

The appetizer course was nearly finished when Ginnie stopped in midsentence and gasped. "Chelsea! Where did you get that gorgeous ring?"

"Greg gave it to me. We're engaged."

Ginnie jumped up and hugged her. "Oh, Chelsea! I'm so thrilled!"

Of course, there were numerous questions about when they would get married, and where, but Chelsea merely told them they hadn't worked out the details.

Finally, the conversation turned to other things. The hamburgers were delicious, and the main thing was that they all had fun together. Everybody had a good laugh over Greg's description of his grammar school principal back in Chicago. "If you even had a bad thought, Mr. Connors would know about it and give you a demerit. Everyone was in mortal terror of the large paddle leaning against his desk. Did he ever use it? He didn't have to. Just the sight of it was all he needed to keep us in line."

Thomas was especially tickled. "I guess times have changed a lot. I wouldn't dare have a paddle in my school. Just the knowledge that it was there would be dangerous, and to use it would tempt someone to sue."

They talked about their plans for the summer. Thomas planned to relax at his family's cottage in Maine, and Ginnie was going to a library convention in Boston. Greg had planned his cross-country tour, but it was now on hold, and Chelsea merely said she had a wedding to plan. "If I have any spare time, I'll do some painting."

Before Greg had asked her to marry him, she had intended

to start an annual visit to interesting places with a trip to Yellowstone. That would have to wait until some other summer.

Later that night, Chelsea thought about their evening. It was fun being with their friends, but even better when she and Greg were alone. She savored his good-night kiss as she turned out the light and went to sleep with a satisfied smile on her face.

fifteen

There were so many decisions to be made. Chelsea and Greg sat in the living room of his house, drinking iced tea and looking through a book of house plans.

Greg didn't push his own ideas on her, even though he might have wanted to. This was just an exploration. "I know it's too much to expect us to like exactly the same things, but I thought we might combine some of the features I like most with some of your favorites and come up with something unique."

"That's an exciting idea if we can get it to work."

"Don't worry. Hal can do anything. He's the most talented architect I've ever met."

Chelsea could already see a house in her mind's eye on the acreage they had just looked at. "I can't imagine a house that wouldn't look wonderful on that gorgeous property." They had driven out to the edge of town, so Greg could show her where he intended to build his dream home. It was a grassy field with a gentle incline, shaded by several large pine trees as well as some scrub oaks.

"I see the house right on the top of that incline," he said.

She agreed that would be perfect, then they returned to his house to make their plans.

"As I see it, if they can start right away, it should be finished by the time we return from our honeymoon."

Chelsea nodded. "It's all a matter of timing. I thought I was organized, but this takes more organizing and decision making than I've ever had to do."

"You can do it. Actually, I'm amazed at how much we already agree on, and compromise is easy when you love someone." He hugged her, and they continued to concentrate on the house plans.

In the week since he'd proposed, they had already decided on a wedding date. It would be at the end of summer, so they could return from their honeymoon in time for the start of school.

Chelsea had known ever since she was sixteen just what her wedding would be like. It would be very traditional. She'd wear a long white gown with a waist-length veil (she even had a scrapbook with pictures of wedding dresses she liked) and carry a bouquet of white roses and stephanotis.

She had already gone to the best dressmaker in New Mill, who measured her and went over all the details with her.

The minister at her church in Stanville had set aside the date she'd asked for, but she had yet to make arrangements for the cake and refreshments for the reception. She did plan to have it at the church, though.

That left the bridesmaids to be contacted and the invitations to be ordered.

Now a new and troubling thought occurred to her. She had never met Greg's family. That's when she realized how quickly she had fallen in love with him. There had been little discussion of his family since he had told her about them the night they had dinner at Barcarolle.

What if she didn't like them? Or, even worse, what if they didn't like her?

It was Greg who finally brought it up again. They had interrupted their planning session to go out to eat. "Do you realize you've never met my family?"

She felt relieved that he had been the one to mention it. "Yes, and it does concern me."

"Let's drive down to Chicago in a couple of days. My mother is anxious to meet you."

She took a deep breath, already nervous. "Okay, I'll be ready."

It took willpower, but she put the thought aside and concentrated on enjoying their dinner. Greg had taken her to a small cafe owned by a friend of his.

Mark had greeted them effusively. "I've been anxious to meet Greg's fiancée. In fact, I believe I saw you at the church chili supper. I intended to visit with you that night, but you got away before I could manage it."

The food was simple and delicious. Mark specialized in down-home cooking, which was very popular in that part of the country. "The meat loaf is just out of the oven, and I think you'll like it." He served it with mashed potatoes, fresh green beans, and rolls.

Chelsea sampled it and nodded. "Without a doubt, that is the best meat loaf I've ever tasted." People were already lined up at the entrance, and it was still early.

"Mark has regulars who eat here every night, singles, elderly folks, and people who just don't want to cook," Greg explained. "I think he's going to have to expand. He's destined for bigger and better things."

"You're right."

While they ate, their conversation naturally returned to their plans. "I still have the invitations to order, the bridesmaids' dresses to decide on, and the caterer to contact," Chelsea said. "You'll need to give me a list of people you want to invite. That's really difficult. I keep thinking of people to add to my list, but there are limits to how many people we can get into that little church, to say nothing of the expense."

"I'll try to hold it down, and you know I'll be glad to help out with the expenses."

"Thanks, but I don't think it will be necessary. I do have some savings, and this isn't going to be a lavish affair. It will actually be quite simple. But I want it to be nice."

After dinner, they returned to his house, and sat out on the patio, drinking coffee. Chelsea looked up at the moon, shining through the leaves of the big plane tree that shaded Greg's backyard. The leaves moved gently in the soft breeze that stirred the fern hanging from the eaves.

"How many couples like us have sat beneath that moon, planning an unknown future together?"

Greg sighed. "Even the early settlers probably felt very much the same way." He was silent, thinking. "How many children do you want?"

"At least two. One of each. How about you?"

"Yes, I'd like a boy and a girl. If we have all one sex, then I think we should stop at four. That's enough." He laughed. "I guess we should be happy with whatever God decides to give us. I know you love children, or you wouldn't be happy teaching."

"I certainly do, and I can't wait to have our first one, even if I get pregnant on our honeymoon."

He took her home early, still protective of her because of her concussion. Her bandage was off, and her hair was carefully combed over the still-tender scar.

His kiss was warm and just as thrilling as the first one had been. She always found it hard to pull away and say good night, and she knew he felt the same way. This night was no different, and she sighed deeply as she watched him walk away. Now she was counting the days.

≈

Chelsea rose early the day they were to leave for Chicago. To her dismay, the first sound she heard was the drip, drip, drip of the rain. She raised the shade and looked out at the dreary landscape. It was a relentless rain, soaking everything in sight.

She showered and dressed in jeans and a T-shirt. Her bag stood in the corner, packed and ready to go. Perhaps they would drive out of the rainstorm before long. She turned on the TV, hoping for a weather report.

The announcer pointed to a map, showing rain covering all of South Dakota and the northern half of Iowa.

She stood at the window, eating a bowl of cereal, trying to convince herself this was not a bad omen. *You silly goose, the rain has nothing to do with whether you like Greg's family, or whether they like you. Just relax.*

Her mood didn't improve until Greg knocked on her door. He was his usual cheerful, upbeat self. "Great day for travel, eh? Are you all ready?"

She did her best to match his mood. "Sure thing."

He lifted her bag. "This thing weighs a ton. Are you taking your entire wardrobe?"

"Women need more stuff," she explained, as she grabbed her purse and turned out the light.

They each held an umbrella as they hurried out to Greg's car.

If this weather bothered Greg, he didn't show it. He very cheerfully turned on some good music, headed out for the highway, and appeared to Chelsea to be perfectly contented. After a while, he turned to her. "You're awfully quiet. Is something wrong?"

"I guess I'm kind of worried about meeting your family."

"Well, don't be. They'll love you, and they're very nice people. Trust me, it will be fine."

They drove most of the day, taking time out for a light lunch, and stopped around 5:30 at a motel in a small town in Iowa.

"I've been here before," Greg assured her. "This one should be just fine."

They had an adequate meal at a fast-food restaurant. "Is your room okay?" Greg asked.

"Sure. Clean and comfortable. The TV works. I'm sure I'll sleep well."

By this time the rain was little more than a drizzle. "I think we've outrun the rain. The rest of the trip should be more pleasant," Greg said.

They were both tired from the long drive, so after dinner he took her back to her room, gave her a tender kiss, and said good night. "We'll get into Chicago about five. I'm sure Mom will have dinner for us, so it will work out just fine."

Chelsea had left out the clothes she wanted to wear into Chicago, so she could be ready quickly in the morning.

When Greg tapped on her door the next morning, she was already showered and dressed. She quickly opened the door. "I must have been more tired than I realized last night. I didn't hear a thing until I awoke this morning."

Greg smiled. "Me, too. It looks like the rain is gone."

They had a bite of breakfast at their motel's continental breakfast room and were soon on their way.

With the beautiful red sunrise, Chelsea's outlook improved. They chatted about their plans once they reached Chicago and listened to music as they drove. The trip that day was less tiring, probably because the weather was nicer.

Traffic increased considerably as they neared the outskirts of Chicago. Greg explained they wouldn't have to go through the city to reach his family's house. "Fortunately, we can turn off the expressway when we reach their outlying town. It isn't far."

Chelsea didn't know what to expect, but she wasn't prepared for the large, attractive houses they passed once they took the turnoff.

"My parents bought this house the year I entered high school. It's more than they need now, but they're happy here."

They pulled into the driveway of a lovely two-story brick home with a well-landscaped lawn. "This is it."

"Very nice," Chelsea murmured.

A pleasant-looking, plump little woman, a little shorter than Chelsea, appeared at the entrance. She broke into a broad grin at the sight of them, and hurried out to the car. "Welcome! I've been watching for you." She gave Greg a big hug.

"Mom, this is Chelsea," Greg said.

His mother took her hand in both of hers and brushed cheeks. "We're so glad to have you," she said.

Greg's father joined them. He was as tall as Greg, but somehow different in appearance. In addition to being older, he had a rougher appearance. "Are you going to stand out there all night?"

"Dad, this is Chelsea." He put his arm around her shoulders possessively. "Don't mind him, hon. He thinks he's tough."

The older man took her hand. "Welcome to our home. Come on in."

Chelsea had the distinct impression Greg's father not only thought he was tough, but he was tough. Perhaps, she imagined, it was because he had managed to survive teamster strikes, bad times of every kind, and come out on top. She had to admire him for it.

The interior of the McCormick home matched the exterior, well-furnished, tastefully decorated, and comfortable. Greg took Chelsea upstairs and showed her the guest room. He put her bag on the luggage rack and gave her a quick kiss. "See, they aren't so bad, are they?"

"They're lovely, Greg. No wonder you turned out so well. Should I change for dinner?"

"Not unless you want to. You look fine. We're not formal. Why don't you come on down? Clint will be here any minute."

His brother came in the front door just as they were coming down the stairs.

He and Greg greeted each other warmly with the brotherly pats on the shoulder and the hearty handshakes one would expect since they didn't see each other very often.

Clint was a good three inches shorter than Greg, with sandy hair and wire-rimmed glasses. He turned to Chelsea. "I've been wanting to meet you. It's high time Greg settled down."

Since he was three years older than Greg, Chelsea wondered if he shouldn't be settling down, too.

She handed Greg's mother a little gift bag containing the last one of her pear preserves, for which Mrs. McCormick thanked her graciously. She declined Chelsea's offer to help put the meal on. "It's very simple. It will be ready before you know it."

Mrs. McCormick had cooked a delicious brisket, which she served with coleslaw and a platter of mixed vegetables. For dessert, there was warm cherry pie topped with ice cream. *No doubt she's catering to Greg's appetite,* Chelsea thought.

The conversation centered around their plans to entertain Chelsea and Greg for the short time they would be there. Since Chelsea had already told Greg she wanted to have lunch with her cousin, Louise, they planned to go into town the next day, where Greg could meet a couple of old friends for lunch. Afterwards, there would be window shopping on Michigan Avenue and dinner at one of Greg's favorite restaurants that night.

On Saturday night, they would have a family dinner at home, and Chelsea would get to meet Clint's friend, Elizabeth. She was astonished to find out they had been going together for two years. "Why don't they get married?" she asked.

"Clint's not one to rush into anything," Greg explained, with a wry grin. "As you may have noticed, we're about as different as two brothers can be. I love him, but I don't always understand him."

Chelsea met Louise at a small restaurant near the art shop where she worked. She was fond of her cousin, but didn't have an opportunity to see her often. Louise was a tall, thin blond, about Chelsea's age, and still unmarried.

"You are coming to the wedding, aren't you?" Chelsea asked. "I want you to be a bridesmaid."

Louise sighed. "You know I'd love to, but I've already made arrangements to take a week off from work and stay with Mother so your mother can be there a week early to help you get ready."

"How thoughtful of you. It would mean a lot to me. You know my prayer circle is praying for Aunt Joanne, and Mother said she is a little better."

"I know. I'm not ready to give up yet."

Louise returned to work after lunch, and Chelsea met Greg to browse down Michigan Avenue, admiring the beautiful and expensive things on display.

"We had better do quite a bit of walking this afternoon," she suggested. "Otherwise, I may have to be measured again for my wedding dress. I tried to have a light lunch, but I know it won't be possible to resist the food tonight."

Indeed, it was not. From tasty appetizers right through the perfectly prepared dinner and ending with the fabulous soufflé, Chelsea ate until she felt sated. It was an evening to remember, surrounded by beautifully dressed diners, in the most luxurious surroundings.

Even so, a quiet evening at home with the family was more than welcome. Chelsea found Elizabeth to be most attractive, conservatively dressed, with lustrous dark hair and a luminous complexion. She and Clint seemed to be well-matched. It was obvious Elizabeth was quiet and reserved, just as Clint was.

On Sunday, they attended church in one of the large, downtown churches. Greg's mother said she thought Chelsea would enjoy it, even though their family usually attended a smaller neighborhood church. It was a beautiful, ornate building, with wonderful stained-glass windows. Still, the service followed the same form as their small church back home.

Afterwards, they had a fabulous brunch at the Ritz-Carlton.

Except for the rainy first day, the weather had been perfect the entire time they were in Chicago. They left early Monday morning amid hugs and kisses all around.

As they sped down the expressway, Chelsea told Greg how much she liked his family. "Your mother is such a darling. She confided in me that she had prayed you would find someone just like me. Isn't that sweet?"

"Yes, that sounds like her. I'm sure they loved you."

As they drove, a feeling of serenity enveloped Chelsea unlike anything she had experienced before. The last tiny bit of doubt had been erased from her mind.

❧

The time sped by in a swirl of activity. Every week they went out to their building site and recorded the progress of their new home. By the time it was finished, they would have a video of it to keep for their children.

Ginnie gave a shower for her, and Chelsea was delighted by all the thoughtful gifts she received.

The final fitting for her dress coincided with the arrival of the bridesmaids' dresses. The days couldn't go by quickly enough for her now. Everything was fitting into place, and the final event, which had originally seemed so impossible to put together, was at hand.

Chelsea's mother arrived with a list of last-minute things to do, only to find that half of them had already been done. "I never realized you were such an organized person," she said admiringly.

"Neither did I, but I'm learning."

Greg's family arrived, and they hosted a lovely rehearsal dinner at Bramwell's Inn.

❧

Finally, the hour was at hand. Chelsea stood in the small room adjacent to the vestibule. Her mother fastened the head-piece on her, which was circled with a small band of seed pearls, from which her veil floated down to her fingertips.

A full-length mirror showed the bride she had dreamed of being, radiant in her becoming white gown. The round neck-line revealed a small strand of pearls, a fitted bodice flowed into a graceful, fuller skirt. Chelsea slowly turned around, admiring her image.

"Oh, it's beautiful, darling," her mother said. "You look absolutely lovely." There was a little crack in her voice, and Chelsea sensed her emotion.

The organ started the anthem, and there was a rustle of activity as the groomsmen and the bridesmaids prepared to enter. Chelsea had chosen very simple long, cream-colored dresses for the bridesmaids.

Now Chelsea picked up her bouquet of white roses and creamy stephanotis, inhaling the heady scent. At this moment, she thought of her late father poignantly. She had decided, under the circumstances, that she would like her mother to give her away. Hope was pleased by this decision, and she looked quite lovely in her beige lace dress.

At the time Chelsea asked her, Hope had said she was sure Chelsea's father would be there in spirit. "You know, the way Greg treats you reminds me of how your father treated me when we were young marrieds."

They hesitated a moment, then they picked up their cue from the music and walked slowly down the aisle.

Chelsea's breath caught in her throat when she saw Greg, looking unbearably handsome, waiting for her at the altar. She swallowed hard, determined not to shed a tear.

The church had taken on a different air, festive with creamy ribbons on the pews, and lit by tall candelabra.

So many thoughts jumbled together in her mind as the Reverend Sanders went through the ceremony. It was all going by so quickly. . . "And do you take this woman, Chelsea Hope Morgan, to be your lawful wedded wife to have and to hold so long as you both shall live?"

Greg's response was strong and clear. "I do."

"And do you, Chelsea Hope Morgan, take Gregory Holliwell McCormick to be your lawful wedded husband, to have and to hold for as long as you both shall live?"

Chelsea sought Greg's gaze, so lovingly centered on her. "I do."

Greg took the ring proferred by his best man, Clint, and slipped it on Chelsea's finger.

"I now pronounce you man and wife." Greg circled her in his arms and gently kissed her.

The music swelled; they turned and walked out arm in arm. Chelsea neither saw nor heard anything else that went on. It was all a blur that somehow concealed the depth of her emotion.

❧

They stood together on the rim of the Grand Canyon, arm in arm, gazing out at the spectacular sight. Sparks as brilliant as the diamond solitaire on her left hand flashed in the reflection of the sunlight.

Soon the colors changed from the reddish glow of the setting sun, to purple and mauve as dusk fell.

Chelsea looked up into Greg's eyes, so full of admiration. "I'm amazed how well our wedding turned out, when you consider I put it together in only three months. Most weddings need at least six months, or even a year."

He smiled. "You operate more like a chairman of the board than a schoolteacher."

"Thanks, I think. You forget this union was the result of a larger plan. I had a little help from the Lord."

He drew her close and his kiss, warm and passionate, ignited a fiery response inside her. His mouth moved over her face and down to her neck as he nuzzled delicious little kisses in every crevice.

Her words sounded a bit breathless. "I think we had better go in before you forget where you are and step back in the wrong direction."

"You're right. Our family doesn't need another concussion. Besides, we don't want to waste a perfectly good honeymoon out here in the cold." The warmth in his voice reflected the love in his eyes.

A Letter To Our Readers

Dear Reader:

In order that we might better contribute to your reading enjoyment, we would appreciate your taking a few minutes to respond to the following questions. We welcome your comments and read each form and letter we receive. When completed, please return to the following:

Rebecca Germany, Fiction Editor
Heartsong Presents
PO Box 719
Uhrichsville, Ohio 44683

1. Did you enjoy reading *The Reluctant Bride?*
   ❑ Very much. I would like to see more books
     by this author!
   ❑ Moderately
     I would have enjoyed it more if _____

   _____

   _____

2. Are you a member of **Heartsong Presents**? Yes ❑ No ❑
   If no, where did you purchase this book? _____

   _____

3. How would you rate, on a scale from 1 (poor) to 5 (superior), the cover design? _____

4. On a scale from 1 (poor) to 10 (superior), please rate the following elements.

   _____ Heroine   _____ Plot

   _____ Hero   _____ Inspirational theme

   _____ Setting   _____ Secondary characters

5. These characters were special because_____

_____

_____

6. How has this book inspired your life?_____

_____

_____

7. What settings would you like to see covered in future **Heartsong Presents** books?_____

_____

_____

8. What are some inspirational themes you would like to see treated in future books?_____

_____

_____

9. Would you be interested in reading other **Heartsong Presents** titles?   Yes ❑   No ❑

10. Please check your age range:
   ❑ Under 18   ❑ 18-24   ❑ 25-34
   ❑ 35-45   ❑ 46-55   ❑ Over 55

11. How many hours per week do you read?_____

Name _____

Occupation _____

Address _____

City _____ State _____ Zip _____

Ah, those homemade,

comforting family dinners around the table. But who has time to make them between carpooling and softball games?

Don't let your busy schedule deter you. This collection of delectable recipes—from the readers and authors of inspirational romances—has been gathered from all over the United States, and even from Greece and Australia.

There are tried and true recipes for every occasion—Crock-Pot meals for busy days, fast desserts for church dinners, rave snacks for after school, holiday gifts for those picky relatives, and much, much more. Over 700 recipes await you! Bring back the joy of treasured moments over good food with the ones you love. So, dust off the china and treat your loved ones (and yourself) to some delicious home cooking.

The Heart's Delight *cookbook has what every family needs—cooking from the heart.*

400 pages, Paperbound, 8" x 5 ³⁄₁₆"

Please send me _____ copies of *Heart's Delight*. I am enclosing $4.97 each. (Please add $1.00 to cover postage and handling per order. OH add 6% tax.)

Send check or money order, no cash or C.O.D.s please.

Name_____

Address _____

City, State, Zip _____

To place a credit card order, call 1-800-847-8270.
Send to: Heartsong Presents Reader Service
PO Box 719, Uhrichsville, OH 44683

········ Presents ········

Great Inspirational Romance at a Great Price!

Heartsong Presents books are inspirational romances in contemporary and historical settings, designed to give you an enjoyable, spirit-lifting reading experience. You can choose wonderfully written titles from some of today's best authors like Veda Boyd Jones, Yvonne Lehman, Tracie Peterson, Debra White Smith, and many others.

When ordering quantities less than twelve, above titles are $2.95 each.
Not all titles may be available at time of order.

SEND TO: **Heartsong Presents** Reader's Service
P.O. Box 719, Uhrichsville, Ohio 44683

Please send me the items checked above. I am enclosing $_____
(please add $1.00 to cover postage per order. OH add 6.25% tax. NJ add 6%.). Send check or money order, no cash or C.O.D.s, please.
To place a credit card order, call 1-800-847-8270.

NAME _____

ADDRESS _____

CITY/STATE _____ ZIP _____

HPS 1-99

Hearts♥ng Presents
Love Stories Are Rated G!

That's for godly, gratifying, and of course, great! If you love a thrilling love story, but don't appreciate the sordidness of some popular paperback romances, **Heartsong Presents** is for you. In fact, **Heartsong Presents** is the *only inspirational romance book club*, the only one featuring love stories where Christian faith is the primary ingredient in a marriage relationship.

Sign up today to receive your first set of four, never before published Christian romances. Send no money now; you will receive a bill with the first shipment. You may cancel at any time without obligation, and if you aren't completely satisfied with any selection, you may return the books for an immediate refund!

Imagine. . .four new romances every four weeks—two historical, two contemporary—with men and women like you who long to meet the one God has chosen as the love of their lives. . .all for the low price of $9.97 postpaid.

To join, simply complete the coupon below and mail to the address provided. **Heartsong Presents** romances are rated G for another reason: They'll arrive *Godspeed!*